The Prince of Denmark

For Marilyn Holderness

che da per li occhi una dolcezza al core

and The Rev. Kevin Morris

dolcissimo padre

amor mi mosse, che mi fa parlare

PREVIOUS BOOKS ON SHAKESPEARE
BY GRAHAM HOLDERNESS

Shakespeare's History (Dublin: Gill and Macmillan, 1985).
Hamlet (Milton Keynes: Open University Press, 1987).
The Shakespeare Myth (Manchester: Manchester University Press, 1988).
Shakespeare: The Play of History (with Nick Potter and John Turner)
    (London: Macmillan, 1988).
Shakespeare in Performance: The Taming of the Shrew
    (Manchester: Manchester University Press, 1989).
Richard II: a Critical Study (Harmondsworth: Penguin, 1989).
Shakespeare Out of Court: dramatisations of court society (with Nick Potter
    and John Turner) (London: Macmillan, 1990).
Romeo and Juliet: a Critical Study (Harmondsworth: Penguin, 1989).
William Shakespeare, Hamlet (with Bryan Loughrey) (Harlow: Longman,
    1990).
Shakespeare Recycled: The Making of Historical Drama
    (Hemel Hempstead: Harvester Wheatsheaf, 1992).
Shakespeare's History Plays: 'Richard II' to 'Henry V' (London: Macmillan,
    1992).
The Tragicall Historie of Hamlet, Prince of Denmarke (1603) (with Bryan
    Loughrey) (Hemel Hempstead: Harvester Wheatsheaf, 1992).
The Merchant of Venice: a Critical Study (Harmondsworth: Penguin, 1993).
Shakespeare: the Histories (London: Macmillan, 2000).
Cultural Shakespeare: essays in the Shakespeare myth
    (Hatfield: University of Hertfordshire Press, 2001)
Visual Shakespeare: essays in film and television
    (Hatfield: University of Hertfordshire Press, 2002)

The Prince of Denmark

⊕

GRAHAM HOLDERNESS

UNIVERSITY OF HERTFORDSHIRE PRESS

Published in Great Britain in 2002 by
University of Hertfordshire Press
Learning and Information Services
University of Hertfordshire
College Lane
Hatfield,
Hertfordshire AL10 9AB

ISBN 1 902806 12 3 case bound

BRITISH LIBRARY CATALOGUING-IN-PUBLICATION DATA
A catalogue record for this book is available from the British Library.

Cover Pictures

Front cover
The Young Martyr, 1855 by Hippolyte Delarche (Paul) (1797–1856)
Lourve, Paris, France/Peter Willi/Bridgeman Art Library
The Anglo-Saxon helmet from the Sutton Hoo excavation, Suffolk
© The British Museum

Rear cover
Scenes from the Bayeux Tapestry
© Reading Museum Sevice (Reading Borough Council). All rights reserved
Reconstruction of a Viking longship off Greenland
© The Gaiaship Foundation/Stifelson Gaiaship

Design by Geoff Green, Cambridge CB4 5RA.
Cover design by John Robertshaw, Harpenden AL5 2JB
Printed in Great Britain by J. W. Arrowsmith Ltd., Bristol BS3 2NT.

Contents

Preface

(From the *Chronicles of Ansgar*, 11th century)

H aving been providentially, by the grace of Our Lord Jesus Christ, delivered from the persecution of the heathen to the sanctuary of this church and the protection of the Holy Emperor, I Ansgar, servant of Christ, offer to his Grace Archbishop of Hamburg-Bremen in this year of Our Lord 1055, this brief history of his work on behalf of the Lord among the Danes.

By the command of the Lord, his grace did send our brethren to sojourn among the pagans, desirous of bringing them to Christ, and of filling their souls with the blessed spirit. These Northmen are among the most stern and obdurate enemies of Christ, their ways filthy with the sins of pride, gluttony, fornication and murder. Against God's express commandment they set up graven images, making blood-sacrifice to Odin and Thor. The gods they worship are gods of violence and revenge. To these heathen divinities they offer not prayers for peace, but importunities for protection in battle. They ask their gods not for grace, but for the rapine and devastation of perpetual war.

All the more miraculous did it seem when his grace Bishop Unni prevailed upon Harald, King of the Danes, to accept Christ, and to protect the Holy Church in Denmark. This king received the prima signatio* *in the year of grace 965, and began forthwith to undertake the Lord's work, building churches and professing the Christian faith. So it is justly written, on his stone of remembrance in Jutland, that*

This Harald was he who made the Danes Christians.

Yet, of Harald's three sons, only the youngest, Claudius, was baptised in the Holy Spirit. This Claudius was a prince of great humility and piety, who loved the company of priests, and eagerly absorbed their doctrine. He grew up studious and learned, understanding both the ways of the Lord, and the minds of men: his learning large, his wit keen, and his intelligence strong and subtle.

His two elder brothers, Svend and Amled, were as like him as shade is like to sun. They were true Northmen, savage and unreclaimed. While their brother prayed in his private chapel, they would wake and carouse, inciting the court to orgies of drunkenness and lechery. Once, at a great feast celebrating King Harald's victory over the English, Svend and Amled dragged their brother from his devotions and forced him to drink until he staggered and vomited. At dawn they mounted their horses and rode to the village, there to subject their slave-women to foul and unclean ravishment, as is their law and custom. Claudius too, helpless with drink, was obliged to serve his turn as a true Dane.

Though a prince of such learning and piety, Claudius was too weak to restrain his brethren when they plotted to overthrow their father. Secretly, Svend and Amled persuaded those wicked Danes who hated God's holy church to support their rebellion. They seized King Harald, and forced him to abdicate his power. The princes brought to their Great Council, or Thing†, which in Denmark determines all matters of state,

---

*   'first signature' = a provisional baptism
†   council, parliament

all such as were only too willing to take the devil's side, and Svend was chosen king. Tribulation than fell indeed on the Lord's church, and a heavy persecution was visited upon His servants in Denmark. King Svend and his brother Amled wasted no time in leading bands of armed warriors in savage raids, sacking and looting the monasteries, burning the churches to the ground. The holy sisters they ravished and sold into slavery, and they butchered the pious brethren. These men dragged Denmark back into the night of ignorance and impious darkness. The people, terrified for their lives, renounced Christ, and turned again to the savage gods of Asgard. The Lord took pity on his servant Ansgar, and delivered me from this persecution, only that I might recount this true history, to the perpetual shame of the Northmen, and to the greater glory of God.

For the vengeance of the Lord, swift or slow, is always sure. Svend lived to be remembered by the Danes as a great king, a warrior who by conquest enriched and extended the Danish power. His league with the King of Norway, Anlaf Tryggvassen, gave him success as far abroad as England. By Anlaf's death, Svend became King of Norway and Denmark.

On Svend's death his brother Amled succeeded to dominion over Denmark and Norway. Amled's claim to Norway was soon disputed by Anlaf's son Fortenbrasse, who thought a younger son of Harald might be more mild and tractable than his fierce brother Svend. But Fortenbrasse soon learned of his error in this, when Amled slew him in single combat on the shores of Norway. So the sons of Harald won worldly glory, and all the lands of Denmark and Norway lay at King Amled's feet. But the Danes could not long escape from the judgement of God.

For after this, Amled himself was slain in his own court by poison. So the wicked godless life of this king and his brother brought Amled to an ignominious death. Thus always is God's judgement dealt harshly to those who disobey his will. And while those who win earthly glory believe they can cheat God's vengeance, their success is granted only that their violent ends, unexpected, may be the more bitter and disappointing.

Claudius at last became King of Denmark and Norway, and the Lord's church was restored in the northern lands. To show his forgiveness of his brothers, though they had dealt so hardly with him, he took to wife his brother's widow Gerutha. Notwithstanding she was his sister, his grace the Archbishop was pleased to bless the union. Claudius ruled justly and well, restoring the crown of Norway to Feng, son of Anlaf Tryggvassen, in exchange for a pledge of perpetual peace.

But this king too did not escape the judgement of God upon his wicked family. The sins of his brothers were visited upon him in the plainest fashion, when his mad nephew Hamlet, son of Amled, slew both Claudius and his own mother Gerutha in the presence of the Danish court, then fell upon his own sword. So the innocent fall beneath the sword of vengeance together with the guilty. With all the sons of Harald and their heirs dead, the Great Council of the Danes welcomed as their king Fortinbras, son of that Fortenbrasse slain by King Amled, who on the death of Anlaf's brother Feng became, as Svend and Amled had been before him, King of Denmark and Norway.

The Prince of Denmark

GENEALOGY

Denmark   Norway

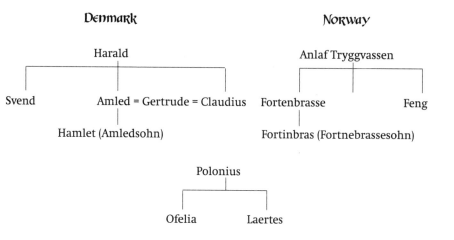

Harald   Anlaf Tryggvassen

Svend   Amled = Gertrude = Claudius   Fortenbrasse   Feng

Hamlet (Amledsohn)   Fortinbras (Fortnebrassesohn)

Polonius

Ofelia   Laertes

Other Characters

Horatio – independent scholar and retainer to Prince Hamlet

Thorsten – Danish military commander and principle retainer to King Amled

Part one

1
Helsingor[*]

June 1050

Remember me.
A thin white froth bubbled from the prince's purpling lips. Horatio held Hamlet's head cradled in his arms, pushing back his wet hair, mopping icy sweat from his forehead.

Hamlet tried to speak, but a spasm of pain doubled his body, knees drawn up to his chin in grotesque foetal reversion. O, o, o, o, o, o. There was no return to that mother's womb, her belly bloated now with the same poison that was swiftly congealing her son's own veins. Beyond her, Laertes had crawled in his agony to face the wall, and lay still in the same doubled position as that which gripped Hamlet. The king's body lay beside Gertrude, on his face, a stain slowly spreading from the wound that had emptied his veins before any venom could begin to circulate from the poisoned point.

The prince's body trembled, his pores exuding a cold sweat. Was this the final agony? But the sudden gripping of a hand told of a will still unprepared to release its hold, of a life not yet ready to surrender its ghost. Horatio

[*] Danish town, better known as Shakespeare's 'Elsinore'

3

leaned closer, straining to hear what the soundlessly moving lips were struggling to voice:

'O good Horatio! what a wounded name ... things standing thus unknown ... shall live behind me!'

Hamlet's hand tightened on Horatio's, as the dying body apprehended, with a cold physical knowledge, its impotence to control the future.

'And I do prophesy ... the election lights on ...' the name was almost spat out: 'Fortinbras!'

This effort of indignation at the prospect of so unworthy a succession, the despair of all aspiration dashed, destroyed what little strength remained to him. His voice, now attenuated in self-pity, whispered the terms of his unprepared and unexpected last will and testament.

'Report me and my cause aright to the unsatisfied ... ' The cracked lips mouthed the words: In this harsh world... draw thy breath in pain... to tell my story! O, o, o, o, o, o!'

Dark blood oozed from his nostrils and the voice was choked into silence. The eyes filmed over with incipient unconsciousness, then they too filled with blood. Hamlet's face was unrecognisable, disfigured in death. The heart had stopped.

Horatio rose to his feet. From outside, the sounds of ragged skirmishing now penetrated his ears. Some of the king's bodyguard must be putting up a token defence against an invader – a detachment, Horatio assumed, of that Norwegian army, on its return from Poland, that had been for some days past camped, peacefully but threateningly, outside the castle. The resistance could not last long: soldiers fight for their lord, not for the sake of fighting. There was no-one left now to command their loyalty, bury their bodies, or avenge their deaths.

The other courtiers had all fled from the scene of carnage, leaving Horatio alone with his sensations. He knelt by Gertrude, piteous of the swollen womb, bitter mockery of motherhood. What unnatural creature would be delivered from that phantom pregnancy?

Suddenly Gertrude's eyes opened. Horatio flinched. Though he had seen the dead walk, nothing had ever surprised him as much as this sudden temporary resurrection. Her eyes seized his with remote intensity, and she spoke, as slowly and clearly as one speaking in a dream.

'The boy. The boy. You must look to the boy.'

In her delirium the dead prince, Horatio thought, is again the baby that once slumbered peacefully against her breast. He glanced at the maimed corpse of her son. What service could he provide for Hamlet now?

Gertrude shook her head. 'No. No. The boy. Find the boy. He must be king.'

She fumbled at her bosom, as if trying to locate something, her fingers tangling with the gold locket on a long gold chain she wore habitually about her neck. Then her eyelids dropped like shutters, and the face, momentarily animated, became again the face of a corpse.

The boy. Horatio had no time to consider her strange words, or to start sifting through possible explanations, before the great hall door banged back, and a detachment of foot soldiers marched quickly in. Their practised gestures of defence were so obviously superfluous, as they caught sight of the scene of slaughter, that their manoeuvres stumbled to a halt. Weapons dropped from nerveless fingers. One man fell to his knees and began to pray. His back to the door, Horatio quickly snapped open the Queen's bodice and slipped from within it a slim package of letters. Snatching the gold locket from her neck, he slid both inside his doublet.

Unhurried, confident, physically imposing in full battle-armour, closely surrounded by his *lith*[*] of personal retainers, Fortinbras entered the hall. He surveyed the destruction, shaking his head slowly from side to side, as though judging an example of poor workmanship.

'Such a sight', he confided to one of his officers, 'becomes the battle-field; but here, shows much amiss'.

Horatio advanced and fell on his knees before the conqueror.

'Great prince', he began, 'as the unhappy survivor of this great – feast of death, it is my sad duty to inform you of all the circumstances ...'

Fortinbras leaned forward and put a hand under Horatio's arm, drawing him to his feet.

'There will be time enough for all that', he said, gently. 'What is your name, my friend? Yes, I have heard of you. You bear the reputation of an honest and intelligent man. The important thing', he went on, his voice becoming more confiding, 'just at this stage, is that we manage to establish peace and stability in Denmark. My troops have secured control of the castle and the town, but there is still a certain amount of resistance – inconvenient to me,

[*]   bodyguard

and fatal to some of your countrymen. I have some rights of memory in this kingdom through my father Fortenbrasse, slain by your former king; and by my grandsire Anlaf Tryg-gvassen of Norway. I intend, in the absence of any other contender, to claim it. Did your king say anything – any-thing at all, you understand – before his death – about the succession?'

'Nothing', said Horatio, his mind elsewhere. 'Not a word'.

'A pity', said Fortinbras, with genuine compunction. 'It would have made things so much easier. Or perhaps', he continued more slowly, taking in the significance of the king's mortal wound, and the bloodstained blade that lay beside Hamlet's body, 'If the son of Amled survived his uncle, he might have given some indication?' – Horatio shook his head – '... a pity', he repeated regretfully. 'But suppose', he suggested, putting an arm around Horatio's shoulder and turning him away from the holocaust of corpses, 'a word had been given? Suppose the Prince had merely mentioned my name in his dying breath? Would we not agree, in the interests of settling the state, that my succession would be infinitely preferable for the health and security of Denmark? I have some good friends in the council of your Thing, but I also have enemies. If the king nominated a successor, and if that nomination were attested by an honest witness such as yourself, then oppo-sition would melt away and we would have all the conven-ience of an undisputed legal succession.'

Then more firmly, 'Do you agree?'

Despite his numbness, Horatio was thinking with furious

swiftness. He was simultaneously trying to analyse the political implications of Fortinbras's words, beginning to piece together the story he would have to tell of Hamlet's tragedy, and seeking to unravel the mystery of the queen's strange testament. Whatever tale he was sworn by his Prince to recount to the future, and whatever quest he had been enjoined by his queen to undertake, he would be helpless to fulfil either from the uncomfortable security of a Norwegian prison. The Danish aristocracy was in too much disarray to contemplate any serious resistance or national recovery; and, above all, as Fortinbras had correctly observed, with the entire regency – king, queen and prince – lying extinct in its own royal blood, there was no obvious alternative contendor for the crown.

Horatio would have to comply, he decided, with Fortinbras's demands. He would have to support the Norwegian accession, and openly speak words chosen for him but which he would, in the long run, be obliged to own. Equivocation, the verbal juggling he despised, was the only course open to him. And Hamlet's last word had indeed been the name of Fortinbras.

'Perhaps my Lord Hamlet may have said something which might be interpreted as encouraging to your princely claim ...'

Fortinbras picked up the hint with alacrity and closed on him with impatient bluntness. 'You would be prepared to speak of this before the Thing?'

Horatio shrugged. 'Yes, my lord, I will support you. But might I be permitted to attach a request of my own in exchange for my freely given allegiance?'

Fortinbras nodded with a slight frown of reservation. Most men he found pliable enough, once they were in his power; but men of intellect often had impractical eccentricities. 'Name them, my friend'.

'May I take the sword of my lord and prince, and keep it as a token of his memory?'

Fortinbras would have laughed out loud had the situation permitted. That a man of such reputed intelligence should seek to impose such an impossible demand! To keep, for present remembrance or future commemoration, the sword of Denmark's heir, the blade that had killed a king?

'You know yourself', said Fortinbras reasonably, 'that what you ask is impossible. You know that sword will be beaten into fragments or dropped into the numberless fathoms of the deepest fjord. My friend, do not ask this of me'.

Horatio shrugged as if surrendering a minor concession. He walked across to the body of Laertes. 'I understand', he murmured. 'This man too was my friend. He slew my prince, though he had just cause. Let me keep his blade'.

Fortinbras glanced at the dead Laertes and seemed for a moment to pause with a slight shock of recognition. He covered the reaction by clapping Horatio's shoulder in brusque camaraderie. 'So be it. We understand one another well. Take the sword'. Then with a gesture of command he signalled to his lith that they should begin to remove the bodies for burial.

Horatio knelt and disentangled Laertes' already stiffening fingers from the hilt of the sword. Let Fortinbras feel secure in his understanding. Horatio certainly understood him. The king-to-be might believe he had the measure of his new man. But Horatio was as determined as had been his former master to ensure that none would ever pluck out the heart of his mystery.

CAUTION

Let a man proceed
With caution when he crosses
A strange threshold:
let him look to left and right.
For how can he know
What enemies wait
To ambush him in the hall?

A man should not be too wise
Or excessively cunning:
Half-wise is best.
No-one can read
The runes of time;
So why not sleep in peace?

A cripple can handle a horse,
A maimed man wield a plough.
A deaf soldier can still fight well.
I'd rather be blind
Than burn on a pyre.
There's nothing the dead can do.

FROM THE HAVAMAL

2
Helsingor

December 1020

What would his brother Svend have done? Try as he might, King Amled could not prevent his mind from presenting and re-presenting the same question. He tossed the letter onto the table among the broken plates and spilled drinking-horns that testified to his initial reaction, on receiving it, of blind overpowering rage.

The king sat alone at the council table in his great castle of Helsingor, having dismissed his retainers to give himself space for deliberation. He had been reading the letter by the light of a fire that spat and crackled under the central smoke hole, since he was too angry to call for lights, and his servants too afraid of their master's rages to intrude on his privacy.

However eloquently his councillors had twisted its words and bent its meaning, the letter continued to spell out one uncompromising meaning: war. With an effort of concentration he focused his eyes in the waning light and read it through again one last time.

Fortenbrasse, son of Anlaf Tryggvassen, to King Amled of Danmark and Norway

To the most noble lord Amled, King of the Danes and Norweyans, from your loyal *jarl** and humble subject Fortenbrasse, greetings.

We Norsemen have honoured you as our overlord, served you as our king, and as our chieftain given you our free allegiance. As your *jarl* I have executed your rule and dispensed your laws, loyally and faithfully. Never have the Norsemen sought to resist your power or to raise arms against your crown.

It is with an appeal to this loyalty, and to your magnanimous justice, that I petition you humbly to set right a great wrong.

When my noble father Anlaf Tryggvassen joined with your illustrious brother Svend to conquer the English, our kingdoms were united in true comradeship. Led by two great warriors, we formed an unmatchable army, greater than any force ever seen before or since.

When my great father fell in battle, that brotherhood of arms was broken. That kingdom that should have descended justly to Anlaf's heir was seized by force. Though Anlaf bore his sword against your common enemies, and even died assisting your cause, even before his warrior spirit had reached the gates of Valhalla, your sword was turned against Anlaf's kin.

Great king, I swear by the memory of my father that I covet nothing that is not mine by right. Return the crown of Norway to me and mine, and a pledge of perpetual peace may be signed between our nations. Once again, as sworn comrades, side by side, Norway and Danmark shall march, together but equal, to conquer the world.

* retainer (cp. 'earl')

13

The gods will not permit injustice to continue
unavenged. If Norway come not to the Norseman, then
the Norseman is sworn enemy to the Dane. If we cannot
resolve this dispute as friends, then it will be decided
between enemies. I, Fortenbrasse, son of Anlaf and rightful heir to the crown of Norway, here pledge that if battle
is needed to secure justice and recover my right, then
battle shall be offered to the King of Danmark by his erst-
while loyal and loving subject

FORTENBRASSE

Fortenbrasse's challenge had arrived at a perilous conjunc-
ture for the young king: the worst crisis he could remember since the three sons of Harald – Svend, Amled and
Claudius – had overthrown their elderly father and seized
the crown. Svend, the elder, who was ratified king by
unanimous endorsement of the *Thing*, had already
become a legend among the Danes for heroism and conquest. But it was his league with the King of Norway, Anlaf
Tryggvassen, that made Svend's name. This powerful
alliance of old enemies enabled the extension of Viking
power as far afield as England. Denmark and Norway were
held together in apparently unbreakable unity by the
charisma of Anlaf's success, both as a leader of men, and
as a conqueror of nations. Bearing in one hand the sword
of war, in the other the olive-branch of peace, Anlaf had
represented a new type of warrior-politician, as plausible
in diplomacy as he was feared on the battlefield. A combination of efficient political order, and murderous ruth-
lessness in the devastation of peaceful communities, had
proven effective in subduing a range of once proud tribes

and nations. Hence Anlaf had been able to disarm both military resistance and political dissent: terrorising armies into enforced passivity, persuading kings into willing co-operation.

Svend, Amled knew only too well, had been a poor successor to his great Norwegian ally. Brave enough on the battlefield, courageous and inspiring as a general, Svend had been as deficient in the arts of peace as he was proficient in the science of war. The alliance had already, in the few years since Anlaf's death, begun to creak audibly at the joints, since Svend had made no attempt to defuse the ethnic tensions between Dane and Norwegian, nor to facilitate compromise between the bickering chiefs on both sides of the border. Nor was Svend able to see, as his father Harald had clearly seen, the potentiality of the Christian church to strengthen kingly power and promote social cohesion. By persecution Svend had suceeded in alienating the missionaries, their Danish converts, and the leaders of that Christian empire which was plainly, once again, becoming the power-base of the European mainland, and with which the Scandinavian kingdoms would eventually be obliged to come to terms.

Well, Svend was dead now, may Odin care for his soul, and Amled had to face the crisis alone. He was a man, take him for all in all, thought Amled: I shall not look upon his like again. Amled had no personal predilection for the new Christian faith, though he had, largely owing to the persuasions of his pious wife Gertrude, accepted the necessity of baptism. But he could see, more clearly than his elder brother had ever seen, how the principles of love and forgiveness promulgated by the church promoted domestic peace and stability, and as such were essential for a kingdom aspiring to serious political power. Denmark faced, Amled had grasped, a stark choice between two avenues of development. The kingdom could continue to exist as a collection of private armies, living on pillage. They could raid and forage, ever further and further abroad, sometimes together, sometimes independently. They could enjoy moments of comradeship in success, but at every crisis would turn against one another in the destabilising violence of feud. Or Denmark could seek the kind of internal unity that had been achieved, by a combination of political craft and Christian evangelism, in other neighbouring kingdoms. With such unity achieved, Denmark could undertake a concerted imperial expansion, as Rome had done, intelligently subduing all nations that fell within the reach of its power.

Amled felt tired. Speculation always wearied and depressed him. The analysis of a situation invariably seemed to produce more alternative possibilities, and obscured all clarity of purpose and decisiveness of action. The business of listening to counsel, patiently hearing the advice of his courtiers and chieftains, inevitably reduced him to frustration. He was aware, as he had never been while his brother lived, of how much he had relied, since they had deposed their father, upon Svend, to take the lead in council, as well as on the battlefield – even though he could never recall the elder brother having an original idea not supplied to him by others, often by Amled himself. He still resented his own lack of confidence in his leadership, and his own impatience with arguments that seemed, *prima facie*, so equally convincing that they cancelled one another out in a vacuum of irresolution.

The Council had split between two incompatible courses of action. The courtiers, led by the chief minister of the crown, Polonius, and supported by Amled's younger brother Claudius, had advocated a peaceful solution, based on compromise and negotiation. Ambassadors should be dispatched immediately to Norway to convey messages of goodwill and amity; to reinforce the basis of the alliance in reciprocal self-interest and mutual advantage; and to offer Fortenbrasse a share in the sovereignty of the two nations. The precise constitutional terms of the arrangement could be worked out formally in due course; the urgent imperative was to indicate to Fortenbrasse that there could be a peaceful path to the realisation of his ambitions. War with Norway, they urged, would destroy the alliance; risk Denmark's independence, curtail the search for profit abroad; and expose both kingdoms to foreign assault.

The chiefs, on the other hand, spoke uncompromisingly – as they always did – for war. Submission to such provocation was unthinkable. Honour demanded that Denmark respond appropriately to a national insult. Diplomatic compromise would send, not only to Fortenbrasse but also to other potential enemies, a clear message that Denmark was weak and vulnerable. The army must be put immediately on full alert, since a pre-emptive invasion could not be ruled out, and preparations undertaken for a march against Norway. Fortenbrasse was no Anlaf Tryggvassen, but a beardless youth, strong in the arm and weak in the head, drunk with ambitious fantasies of replicating his father's greatness.

In one sense the choice was clear, and Amled was not afraid to take the decision. But he mistrusted equally the spurts of violent anger that jetted in his blood each time he glanced at Fortenbrasse's letter; and the attractive clarity of the arguments for peace that appealed so strongly to his reason and political sense. He knew that on occasions the violent impulses of the blood needed subordinating to intelligent analysis and rational forbearance. On the other hand, the crystalline beauty of logical counsel also held its own seductive enchantment, and Amled could think of many occasions when what had passed for reason proved, eventually, to be mere cowardice, and where the decisive action that was shirked would have been the only true and principled response.

What would Svend have done? There would have been, Amled reflected, not a second's hesitation in his brother's mind. But Amled had had the leisure, while the elder brother had held the responsibility of rule, to observe, to listen and to think. In Anlaf Tryggvassen he had perceived a new kind of leader, and in the alliance he had glimpsed the possibility of a new kind of state. Svend might well have crushed Fortenbrasse, and terrorised the Norwegians into subjection, by a devastating lightning assault. But then in undertaking such an action, Svend would also have forfeited a chance of bringing a new Denmark that fraction closer to realisation.

Amled scraped back his stool and rose from the table. His limbs demanding physical exertion, he paced up and down the length of the hall. The dogs scattered before him, fearing the violence of his anxiety and anger. He paused by a window and stared, through drizzling darkness, to where a narrow grey sea lay sluggishly beneath winter mists, separating Denmark from Sweden and Norway. In his hard blue eyes could be glimpsed, as he thought in detail about the physical ardours of a campaign, the vicious white coldness of the northern winter. For a brief moment the painful thought of his young wife, who was about to be delivered of their first child, flashed across his mind, and was as quickly dispelled.

Amled seemed to make up his mind. Then he shouted for attendance and sent a terrified *traell** scuttling in search of the Lord Thorsten. Minutes later, Thorsten entered the hall, fell to his knees before the king, and kissed his hand in formal salutation. Though but a few years older than Amled, Thorsten always gave an impression of seniority and experience. Born into the ranks of the Danish aristocracy, his ancestral grandsires the *jarls* of Jutland, he had automatically assumed the highest rank in the military oligarchy. Wasting no time in the formal education that was becoming increasingly *de rigeur* for the young men of his class, he had begun his military training, under the close personal supervision of King Harald himself, almost as soon as he could walk.

Thorsten had deliberately absented himself from the

---

* servant, slave (cp. 'Thrall')

Council meeting in open contempt for the processes of debate and discussion and as an unmistakable indication that as far as he was concerned there could be nothing to talk about. He represented the traditional values of the Viking aristocracy in their purest form, quietly ignoring all new developments in thought and culture, fashion and education. He knew of no gods greater than Thor and Odin, no service more distinguished than loyalty to his sovereign and no way of life more honourable than that of the soldier. Amled knew that Thorsten would have as little doubt as would Svend about how to respond to Fortenbrasse's challenge, and knew that there would have been no point in consulting him except on the basis of a firm decision to accept. But he counted on the professional warrior possessing sufficient tactical intelligence to be able to show him, once he had settled on his course of action, how to bring it to a successful conclusion.

Incongruously dressed for the court in surcoat and mail, Thorsten stood before the king, arms folded, a mocking smile creasing his mouth under the heavy moustache. He too was well aware that the young king (as he always thought of Amled) must, before seeking his opinion, have determined to take on Fortenbrasse, and to seek combat. Thorsten called for drink and led the king back to the Council-table. The two men sat opposite one another, taking long draughts from their drinking horns and speaking in low voices, as the winter shadows deepened outside, and as a thick darkness, broken only by the red light of the dying fire, fell within the hall.

BATTLE

As the conflict grew closer,
Keen for the struggle, steadfast swordsmen
Scented success, glory of battle
Lay in each one's grasp. But every man knew
That a share of those shieldsmen
Were doomed for destruction, marked
For the massacre, fated to fall.
Hubbub of battle loudly arose. Raucous the raven,
For carrion circling. Expectant the eagle,
Eager for prey. Earth rang with the uproar.
Then from hard hands flew file-hardened lances,
Savagely-sharpened spearpoints were flung.
Bowstrings were busy, sword struck against shield.
Bitter the battle: on all sides
Soldiers were slaughtered, young lads laid low.

FROM THE BATTLE OF MALDON

3
Norway

December 1020

The Danes' dragon ships were shelved on the Norwegian ice where the warriors had beached them under cover of darkness. The vessels afforded a flank of protection to the Danish troops, placing them out of reach for arrow and javelin. Beyond the ships they could see a bristling line of Norwegian spears rising from a perfectly-disciplined shield-wall of brightly painted, red and yellow linden boards. Beyond, where the ground rose, thickly serried ranks of men could be seen defending the king's *heorthwerod**, who in turn protected the royal standard and the king's person. Somewhere, invisible within a wall of warriors, would be Fortenbrasse himself.

Amled was positioned behind his infantry and deep within the iron ring of his own *heorthwerod*, on the very edge of the ice-sheathed strand of Grimstad. His black dragon-ship rode at anchor, ready if need be to snatch the king from shore and row him swiftly out to sea and safety. For every man, in each army, firmly believed that the most disgraceful and dishonourable action any man could

---

* 'home troop' = bodyguard

commit was to leave a battlefield alive after his lord had been killed. To defend the life of the sovereign, and to annihilate the enemy, were the twin and equal imperatives in the Scandinavian warrior code.

Thorsten stood in the prow of the ship, from which vantage point he could see the whole field. He would be acting as field commander, executing the king's orders, and if necessary managing his defence and escape. Above his head flapped the proud black and gold crown motif of the Danish banner.

In stillness and silence the two armies faced one another. The cold bit through their woollen tunics and closely forged iron mail shirts. The shining air, bright with the incandescence of a low and ruddy winter sun, seemed to shiver with fear.

Then from a gap in the shield wall stepped a warrior, clad in the livery of the Norwegian royal house. This man was the officially appointed bearer of the *beotword*[*], a formal speech of challenge which always preceded a battle, and was designed to enrage and humiliate the enemy. The deep percussion of a drum signalled that the *beotword* was about to be delivered. The herald began to declaim his message, chanting the formal language in time with the drum's pounding.

> 'Hear you, seafarers, what the Norsemen say!
> This is our land, our fathers' birthright,
> won and defended by the might of our swords.
> Here we stand, ready to resist,
> determined never to kneel in surrender.

[*] challenge

Hear my words, Amled, bastard son
of Harald the Dane:
thief of lands, robber of thrones!
Let Norsemen rule where Norsefolk dwell.
Fortenbrasse, Anlaf's son,
here claims his right where his father reigned.
> Return now, Danes, to your Danish lands;
> take back to the Danes your dragon-ships
unburnt, your bodies still unpierced
by the hungry points
of our ice-cold spears'.

His message delivered, the herald delivered a respectful bow and slipped back into the ranks behind the safety of the shieldwall.

The Danes stood in silence, betraying no reaction to the enemy. At a sign from Thorsten, a Danish herald emerged from the front line to declaim a similar message of defiance: which reaffirmed Amled's sovereignty, by right of succession, over Norway, rejected as illegal and unjustified Fortenbrasse's claim, and poured scorn on the strength of his army. The Danish *beotword* was an unconditional ultimatum: no negotiation, no compromise, no surrender. Fight, or die.

Again, silence fell, apart from a faint murmur of voices from beneath the Norwegian royal standard, as Fortenbrasse's advisers discussed the situation. Pitched battle was, from a strategic point of view, always best avoided, since in the mêlée of hand-to-hand fighting, casualties were so grievously heavy. But here there seemed, in the light of Amled's *beotword*, no space at all for manoeuvre. Continuing delay, and the persistent mutter of voices from Fortenbrasse's position, began to suggest some irresolution among the Norwegian high command. It was clear to Amled that there could be no consensus within the enemy camp and that some, at least, of the enemy commanders must lack confidence in their leader. He glanced back at Thorsten, watching attentively from the prow of the dragon-ship. Evidently in reply to the king's inquisitive glance, Thorsten gestured with a clenched fist towards the enemy.

A shock-tremor ran along the Norwegian lines and a thousand men gasped simultaneously in astonishment. At the centre of the Danish shield wall appeared a space, out from which stepped, tall in his black armour and long sur-coat, silver-painted shield in his left hand, in his right a short iron poleaxe, King Amled himself, inexplicably stepping clear of his own front line defences and walking unhesitatingly towards the enemy. Close behind, trotting to keep pace with his long strides, came the warriors of his *heorthwerod*, flanking him on both sides and covering the rear, but making no attempt to interpose between their sovereign and immediate danger. Presently Amled was within a lance's throw of the enemy defences, placing himself with apparent recklessness in suicidal peril.

The king stopped and, projecting his voice towards the hillock on which he knew Fortenbrasse to be placed, uttered with a clear, ringing voice, the single word:

'*Holmganga!*'[*]

The moment was held by a thick, palpable silence. '*Holmganga*' meant a duel, so called because it was usually

[*]   single combat

fought on the seclusion of an isolated island. Against all contemporary conventions of warfare, but invoking an ancient code of Viking chivalry, Amled had challenged Fortenbrasse to single combat to the death.

Initially there was no response from the Norwegian ranks. Amled waited a moment, his pale face gathering, between the bronze cheek-plates of his helmet, a red rash of indignant anger. Raising his axe high above his head, he smashed it down with astounding force onto the thick-ribbed veins of ice that swirled at his feet. The crash of the impact echoed from headland to headland, and splintering shards of ice flew through the thin bright air.

Immediately there appeared some consternation in the Norwegian ranks, some tightly contained jostling and shouldering movement, accompanied by cries of anger and alarm. Then bursting out from the mêlée of men who had tried to contain him, Fortenbrasse came stumbling and sliding through the shield wall, skidding to a stop opposite Amled. His face was concealed by the noseguard of his conical helmet, but his eyes glared a dangerous red-ness of anger, and his chest heaved with the exertion of his escape.

Amled made no movement, but simply stood confronting his challenger, patiently waiting for Fortenbrasse to compose himself. The red colour drained from his cheeks and his face regained its natural pallor. His cold blue eyes were held unwavering on Fortenbrasse's face.

The two armies now stood helplessly by, unable to take any part in the action. Against all counsel, and in defiance of all strategic wisdom, Fortenbrasse had found himself unable to resist Amled's direct and personal challenge to single combat. The king and the prince were now a law unto themselves, isolated in the violence of their enmity, two black-clad figures silhouetted in sharp relief against the flat grey ice. The two armies, each now fanned out in a long semi-circle, inscribed the circular arena of their contention, and awaited the outcome of a combat that would determine, in one way or another, all their futures.

Each of the two contenders turned his left shoulder towards the other, dropping the shield into defensive position, and with his right hand tested the weight of his weapon. Fortenbrasse handled a long, heavy sword, Amled lightly twirled his short poleaxe. Slowly they circled one another, like gladiators in the Roman Coliseum, each pair of eyes locked into the other's. Fortenbrasse was a head shorter than Amled but hoped to make up the distance by the length of his sword and by the legendary strength of the right arm that held it, that 'strong arm' from which his name derived. Thorsten had advised Amled that Fortenbrasse, whose fighting talents lay more in strength than in stamina, would try to wager everything on a single blow, powerful enough to cut through shield, helmet and armour. If Amled could withstand that first blow, and catch Fortenbrasse offguard, then the victory could be his. 'Never take your eyes off his right hand,' the veteran warrior had repeated, over and over again. 'Be ready for that first blow. Remember why he goes by the name of Fortenbrasse.'

Fortenbrasse feinted with his shield, but Amled showed no reaction. Through expressionless eyes, he was watching

Fortenbrasse's right hand, the fingers of which remained relaxed on the hilt of the sword, indicating no immediate intention of striking. Fortenbrasse feinted again, this time more aggressively; but Amled stood his ground. On the third feint, as the edges of their shields clapped together, Fortenbrasse's sword seemed to flower from his wrist with incredible swiftness, weaving a kaleidoscope of light in the frosty air, and cut irresistibly downwards towards Amled's head. But the young king had observed Fortenbrasse's fingers tighten on his sword hilt and, in anticipation of the assault, stepped a pace back and thrust his shield forward.

Taking the blow on his shield, Amled used it to parry the weapon away to his left. Though the solid wooden linden-board was cleft in two by the force of the impact, Amled spared no attention to its loss. For while the sword was sliding sideways over the broken shield face, he rose on the balls of his feet, and used his long reach to drop over the rim of Fortenbrasse's shield a single, devastating, thunderous blow with his axe, a vicious chop that sliced through iron and bone and brain as easily as it had cut through the crust of ice that rimed the Norwegian shore. His head unseamed from crown to chin, he crumpled to the ground in a shapeless heap of blood and bone, bright chips of wood from Amled's fractured shield falling like petals on his lifeless corpse.

Pausing only to draw a quick, deep breath, Amled raised his eyes towards the Norwegian lines, ready to resume defensive formation to repel the expected assault. Fortenbrasse's retainers could not without dishonour retire from the battle field where their lord lay slain. But what Amled saw made him doubt the truth of what his eyes told him; or at last disbelieve in the occurrence of such overwhelming good luck. Should Fortenbrasse agree to fight in single combat against the advice of his council, Thorsten had explained, the Norwegians could in principle disown him, and offer their allegiance to another lord, freed by the commander's folly from their duty of allegiance to the death.

Every soldier of the Norwegian army knelt on one knee, weapons peacefully lowered, heads respectfully bowed as they offered their loyalty to that Amled who had proven himself, both in justice and in power, their rightful king. Amled glanced back to the shoreline to see Thorsten signalling to the Danish troops that the day was theirs.

It was finished. And in this way our valiant Amled (for so this side of our known world esteemed him) did slay this Fortenbrasse.

4
Helsingor

December 1020

A t King Amled's request, a bed had been made up for his wife Gertrude in a corner of the Great Hall of

Helsingor castle. Thus while the king presided over the tri-
umphal banquet, distributing gifts to his commanders,
and accepting their reaffirmations of loyalty, he could
look across and regard, with pleasure, the white face of
his wife, still exhausted by a painful labour, and the little
blonde head of his new born son, wrapped tightly in fine
linen cloths, and held securely against his mother's
breast.

Nothing other than a fate woven by the *Norns*[*] themselves could explain the young Hamlet's birth on the very
same day that his father overcame Fortenbrasse on the
shores of Norway. Victory had become even sweeter to the
taste when it became apparent that the kingdom so ably
defended was held in trust for the inheritance of Amled's
heir.

At the foot of the banqueting table, the *scop*[†] quietly
strummed his harp and in a mellifluous voice sang a song
already composed to celebrate the great victory of the
mighty king, Amled the Dane.

> 'As when a dragon-ship, driven to north
> By whirling winds off Iceland's coast,
> Blown by the blast through boiling seas,
> Ruptures its keel on a hidden rock,
> Shatters its prow in splintering shafts,
> So Fortenbrasse,
> Split like a ship from stem to stern,
> Fell with a shock on the icy strand.
>
> High his hand the hero raised,
> High in triumph above his head;
> Low his foe lay at his feet,

[*] the fates in Scandinavian mythology
[†] court poet, singer

His vanity mastered, vanquished his might.
So the Lord smiled on Amled his servant
Gave him the day for the deeds of his life:
Punished the proud man with pains of death.

Beasts die, kinsmen die:
    man is mortal.
But a good man's name
    lives for ever.
Beasts die, kinsmen die:
    man is mortal.
But one thing lives;
    the fame of a great deed'.

Excusing himself to his guests, Amled walked over to his queen's bed, and sat down by her side. Few Viking lords were as affectionate towards their consorts as was Amled; few indeed remaining satisfied with one wife, preferring to continue the polygamous associations which, though frowned on by the church, continued to remain sanctioned by Germanic tradition. Amled had forsworn all other women when he took Gertrude to wife, devoting what little time remained from warfare and politics to securing her happiness and comfort. His love was of that dignity, that it went hand in hand even with the vow he made to her in marriage. As he stroked Gertrude's hair, and watched the sleeping head of his infant son, the words of the *scop*'s heroic lay began to echo in his ears. He began, dimly, to see himself, for the first time, as a character in history, one whose reputation and achievement would provide for his son a strong basis for the exercise of responsible power and prudent rule. Softly he uttered the boy's name: 'Hamlet'. The prince should be a warrior like his father, but also trained in all the modern arts and sciences, educated in all wisdom and knowledge. He would be gifted with everything necessary to sustain a long and successful reign: education, courtliness, power.

Glancing back to the banqueting table where his comrades and followers were alight with raucous enjoyment, he observed his brother, Claudius, his expression thoughtful, also watching the sleeping baby. Catching Amled's eye, Claudius smiled and raised a drinking horn as if to wish the youngster long life and health. But when Amled's gaze returned to his sleeping heir, the smile drained from Claudius' lips, and the serious expression again clouded his face. For a long time he stared deep into his drinking cup, as if trying to read, in the remaining dregs of liquor, some portent, sweet or bitter, from the inscrutable runes of time.

TRANSIT

Since no-one's so knowing
As to deem his departure
No matter of moment, consider this case
In advance of your voyage,
Breeze at the back of you, black sky
Before; how God the good
And within you the wickedness
Will weigh at the dawning
Of death's dark day.

FROM BEDE'S DEATH SONG

5
Helsingor

January 1050

Though the morning had begun with a sharp breath of daybreak and a powdering of frost, a low winter sun had warmed through the old yellow stones of the orchard wall and it was pleasant to walk there within the enclosed space of the castle gardens, between the neatly planted rows of fruit trees that were already beginning to sprout early signs of premature budding. Through a low arch at the end of the walkway, Amled, now an elderly man, could enter a plantation that grew thick and dark with abundant evergreen: polished leaves and toxic red berries of holly, feathery fronds of fir, sweet rough resinous bark of pine showing yellow through the bristling green darkness. Here the walkway ended in a fenced terrace with a wide prospect of the sea; and here the season's sharp chill, in the form of a cutting land-ward breeze that nipped round a headland and swung across the promontory, caught the old king unawares, stinging his grizzled cheeks and shaking sudden water from his rheumy eyes. He furled his cloak more tightly around his body, still tall, but lean and sculpted to the bone by age, to keep out the chill. As quickly as he could, he retraced his steps through the plantation and re-entered the relative warmth of the orchard, that walled and sheltered sun-trap which caught and held, as in a bowl, the thin sweetness of the January sun.

As a young man he had, whenever at leisure, paced vigorously around the plantation, through the extensive shrubberies and formal gardens, along the terraced path-ways cut into the cliff face, until tired enough to stretch himself on a couch in his favourite corner of the orchard, under a wall bright with the spreading of vari-coloured ivy and sweet with the tangling tendrils of honey-suckle, for an hour of dreamless slumber. Even in the winter season this was his custom always of the afternoon: inured by the hardness of war and travel, he slept out-doors as well in the January cold as in the heat of midsum-mer. Now, as his years advanced, so his walks shortened and slowed, but his afternoon nap under the old orchard wall remained with him an unbreakable habit. If the winter air bit shrewdly into his old bones, a *traell* would sling a great bearskin over him, and his sleep would be the more peaceful, under that close-fitting pelt of animal warmth, for the fresh sea air he could feel drawn chill-ingly into his lungs.

Today, though, he was able to enjoy a temporary, unex-pected warmth that took the sharp edge off the season and momentarily forestalled the great whiteness of the winter that waited, its prospect tangibly present in the smallest rustle of wind, quietly at its back. This midwinter spring nonetheless stirred the birds to whistle and chatter, provoked a few premature flowers to put forth tentative blossoms and made the king's blood sing with an unaccustomed lightness of heart.

He was a happy old man. As he composed himself to sleep, he turned over in his mind the many blessings of good fortune for which he could be thankful. His reign had been relatively free from turbulence and instability, a quiet and productive time during which, he felt, Denmark had matured and developed as a nation and a commonwealth. His decisive crushing of the Norwegian threat by the killing of Fortenbrasse had established his reputation among all his neighbouring rulers and guaranteed for a generation Denmark's freedom from assault. Amled had continued Anlaf's policy of promoting colonisation rather than practising piracy and, as a consequence, had succeeded in making of England a tributary nation, bloodlessly delivering to Denmark's coffers a regular income that would formerly have required immense resources to secure.

Amled also derived no little satisfaction from the fact that he had to some extent reshaped the role of ruler among his steadfastly loyal, but fierce and intractable, subjects, having shown them, by the example of his own success, that more is required of a king than personal bravery and indomitable courage in war. Amled had shown beyond any doubt, by the slaying of Fortenbrasse, that he could readily assume the warrior role so capably filled before him by Harald and Svend. But on the basis of that heroic success Amled had done whatever he could to demonstrate to his countrymen the value of statecraft and political intelligence, and to justify his own belief in the interdependence of strength and cunning, showing in practice that often more could be gained from persuasion and trust, than from terror and devastation.

His son, Hamlet, away at school in Wittenberg, would complete this process of modernising the Danish crown and state. Amled had declared the baby prince his heir immediately on his return from the defeat of Fortenbrasse, taking full advantage, in the bright sunrise of victory, of a moment of maximum power. Later, as his knowledge of constitutional developments across Europe grew and his political understanding matured, he was able to congratulate himself on having foreseen the coming importance of the dynastic principle, the inevitable supersession of elective monarchy by hereditary succession. The system appealed to the Danes mainly because of their strong attachment to notions of hereditary courage – they naturally liked to think of the vigorous blood of a hero running vividly in the veins of his son. For rulers like Amled, the prospect of dynastic continuity held out the promise of a stable and predictable evolution, providing precious time and space for planning, influencing, controlling the future, securing as never before a firmer grip on the process of history.

Though the king's nomination of a successor could not automatically over rule the elective powers of the *Thing*, the sovereign's will would, unless there were some strong and self-evident reason against the candidate, in practice be very persuasive. And in settling the succession on an infant, Amled offered his prominent courtiers and chiefs an opportunity of participating in the education of the prince who would eventually rule over them, their children and their country. Thus Hamlet, from an early age, benefited from the best and most comprehensive education a prince could receive. With a warrior like Thorsten to teach him both the physical skills of battle and the arts of military strategy; a learned courtier like Polonius to manage his classical education in the ancient languages, and in politics and law; and his pious uncle Claudius to induct him into the complexities of scholastic theology, the ethics of practical government, and the sophisticated culture of the modern court, Hamlet was able to develop competencies in all the disciplines of contemporary art and science.

From the warrior Thorsten Hamlet had absorbed a deep and lasting respect for the ancient code of Germanic chivalry. He could see, in its haughty lineaments, both the nobility of those antique values of loyalty and service, personal uprightness and dignity; and the barbarity of their vindictiveness, the extravagance of their sensitivity to personal injury and family dishonour. From the king's chief minister, Polonius, he received a firm grounding in classical education, mastering the basics of Latin and Greek, struggling with the difficulty and dullness of Roman law, reading voraciously in the history and legend of those great vanished civilisations. From his uncle Claudius, the most subtle of all his tutors, Hamlet acquired an education in theology, with its sophisticated nominalist methodology the most enduring and illuminating of all his studies. Claudius's humanist world-view combined a breathtaking confidence in the potentiality of Christian man to unravel the mysteries of the universe, with a deep and dark scepticism about the inscrutability of divine providence. On the one hand, man was capable of conquering nature and sharing in the sovereign glory of God; on the other, man stood in the role of hopeless, perpetually disenchanted seeker after some arcane and hidden secret knowledge. Both views of human nature were replicated in Claudius's theory of politics, since to emulate the glory of God on earth was the responsibility of the king; while the king's subjects should be encouraged to see themselves as eternally benighted by ignorance and superstition. Hence they would always be reliant on others, the rulers and the clergy, to explicate the nature of things and to control the bewildering incoherence of the world. Thus while the king would stand in glory, God's image, noble in reason, infinite in faculty, at the centre of the created universe; the king's subjects, by corollary, would sink to little more than a mere quintessence of dust.

Hamlet uncritically digested this dualism of faith and scepticism: the awesome magnitude of a king's responsibility, as God's vice-regent, the deputy elected by the Lord; and the cynical opportunism that deliberately set out to trap the minds of the people in labyrinthine corridors of unresolved curiosity and unsolved speculation. On the other hand, he could clearly perceive its fundamental contradictions. Brought up partially in the naivety of the heroic ideal, he tended to recoil from the machievellianism that justified the use of secret intelligence and covert operations. At the same time, the manifold possibilities for benevolent rule opened up by the new politics persuaded him to recognise the limitations of the chivalric warrior code and to appreciate the potentialities of government, by the educated few, of the barbaric and superstitious many.

It caused Amled some pain to watch his son grow up under the influence of these new ideas, since he knew that Hamlet would inevitably become less and less like his father. But the project of the prince's education was of the king's own manufacture, and Amled was resigned to the losses entailed. Though as a boy, Hamlet had accompanied his father on military campaigns, and had been from an early age trained to the disciplines of war, inured to the atmosphere of the camp and familiar, from a distance, with the terror and excitement of the battle field, Amled had no intention of bringing up his son as a warrior. Never again, he had vowed to himself, would a king of Denmark enact so foolhardy and imprudent a gesture as to engage with an adversary in single combat. Though his duel with Fortenbrasse had become the stuff of legend, and though the Danes preserved that victory in memory as a focal point of national glory, Amled was determined that it would remain where heroic legend belonged, in the past, and would never be repeated in the present or the future of Denmark. It followed that his son's education should be concentrated on culture and civilisation, on the arts of government rather than the science of war: on military strategy rather than weapons training; on politics and philosophy rather than the skills of physical combat; on the principles of statecraft and the techniques of diplomacy, rather than on the rules of engagement and the values of the *comitatus*[*].

Dispatching Hamlet to university in Wittenberg had finally drawn a line under the warrior kingdom of Denmark, and signalled that the future would see a new style of sovereignty. Amled's own education had been a tough training in conflict, conducted against the stubborn rocks of England and the ice-fanged shores of Norway. His son's development would take its shape from the flowering culture of European civilisation, rather than remaining cramped within the iron-clad antiquity of the barbarian north.

Yes, his son would do well, and carry on the work of modernising Denmark and bringing it into the new Europe not as a poor relation but as a nation of power and influence. He would inherit the mantle of Amled's power, but would employ it far more wisely and to more significant effect than Amled had been able to do. And when all was said, should unavoidable conflict arise, he was confident that his clever and courageous son Hamlet, supported by wise chiefs and the bravest of fighting men, would ably defend Denmark against its enemies. Why, Amled reflected, with a father's venial pride in his son's capabilities, in the exercise yard, where he was continually in practice, Hamlet regularly beat all his peers in simulated combat with sword and lance. Should another duel with another Fortenbrasse become an unavoidable necessity ...

Amled put aside these impulses of nostalgia that

[*]   regiment

betrayed his deep affection for the ancient times and for the securities of the old warrior culture. To dispel the anxieties that inevitably arose in any contemplation of the future, he thought of Gertrude, who always appeared in his mind's eye as he drifted off to sleep. Still as beautiful as ever, she continued to represent to him, as she always had, all the pleasures and potentialities of womanhood. Even now, in their late middle age, her body remained for him an inexhaustible reservoir of sensation and fulfilment. Still he would look at her, as she sat at the feast table, presiding over a banquet with all the dignity of a royal hostess, her hair hanging loose and unbraided in the new French fashion, her white gown cut décolleté, to show off both the diamonds that sparkled at her neck, and the elusive curves of her breasts, talking with animation to some ambassador or foreign dignitary, seducing rapt attention with every sparkling smile and with each vivacious word.

Amled's breath would catch in his throat as he realised again, with inexplicably repetitious wonder, that in a few hours they would be alone together in her chamber and she would be shedding her gown as a flower at night sheds its petals, revealing her creamy body and limbs, though thickened from the thin white girl's body he had first embraced, still voluptuous, and rich with a sheen of sensuality; her breasts, though tugged downwards many years before by the importunate suckling of her imperious young son, still shapely and full; the tuft of dark hair between her legs a deliciously incongruous maculation on her otherwise smooth and unblemished skin.

And so King Amled drifted, in the comfort and security of his orchard, softly and smilingly into the pleasure of his afternoon sleep. He was indeed a happy old man.

His daytime sleep had always remained unperturbed by dreams: but on this day he suddenly started awake from a nightmare that had struck at his deepest fears and seemed still to hold him fast in its strange paralysis, his ears stopped in a submarine silence, his limbs stretched inert in a helpless lethargy, only his eyes, wide open in terror, helpless to shut out the recollection of the pageant of tragedy that had seemed to unfold before him.

In his dream he had been lying here on his accustomed couch and Gertrude had come to him, as she sometimes did, her eyes alight with desire, her lips parted in passion. With a serpent's sinuous grace she had slithered under his bearskin cover, pressed her breasts flat against his chest, and eased herself onto his slumbering erection. Inside she was hot and wet, scalding his sensitive skin, pressing his nerves to a delirium of sensation, quickly wrenching the seed out of him so that his stiffness melted like a spent candle in a dribbling trickle of molten wax. She clung on to the hard root of his penis, crooning and rocking, rubbing and frotting herself to a shivering spasm of autonomous and self-contained passion. Exhausted, he felt her slide off his wet body and disappear from view.

His eyes re-opened and there standing before him was Claudius, his face pale with sadness and pity. He made the sign of the cross over his sleeping brother and slowly backed away, his eyes remaining fixed on Amled's face. Then Gertrude was standing behind Claudius, dressed formally in a black gown as if for some ceremony of mourning. Both stared at Amled with expressionless faces, but at the same time conversed inaudibly with one another. Then they turned to one another and kissed, long and deeply, Claudius holding Gertrude tightly about the waist, Gertrude's arms hanging loosely behind her back.

Amled fought to move his arms and struggled to speak; but his limbs were as if paralysed and his mouth struck dumb. He closed his eyes to shut out the dreadful tableau of usurpation and betrayal. When he opened them again the figures were gone, but he himself was drowning, a green sea-swell filling his vision, the noise of the surf crackling and chafing in his ears. The terror of suffocation gripped his stinging nose and clamped around his burning throat. With an immense effort of will, using the last reserves of his strength, he hauled himself awake.

The orchard of his waking vision, though deserted, was little different from the orchard of his dream. The loud running of the surge still hissed in his deaf ears, and his limbs still sprawled in nerveless inertia. Looking down at his hands, he perceived with horror that they were silvered with some hideous tetter, forming on the surface of his smooth skin a vile and loathsome crust. O, horrible! He felt the sensation, within his body, of some foreign, living substance: first coursing like quicksilver through his veins; then slowly curdling like milk; then clotting and clogging to block his arteries and to stop the circulation, through all the natural gates and alleys of the body, of his thin and wholesome blood. Then he knew only too well what was happening.

Cut off, even in the blossoms of his sin. His vision clouded and darkened. Words of confession strangled in his throat, and there was none there to give him absolution. No reckoning made, but sent to his account. Inwardly he called on Odin and Freya, but no custodial ravens flocked to help him, and no Valkyries came to lift and receive his corpse. With all his imperfections on his head.

Adieu, adieu, adieu. Remember me.

6
Helsingor

June 1050

Horatio sat opposite Fortinbras, eyes downcast, preoccupied with his own thoughts, but acutely aware of the other man's movements and reactions, as he slowly perused the thin sheaf of documents Horatio had surrendered to him. Fortinbras had asked for information about Hamlet's absence between the king's dispatching him to England and his return to Denmark alone. This was the one space of time, Horatio supposed, when Hamlet was temporarily free, both from the scrutiny of Claudius's agents (whose records, carefully filed among the state papers, Fortinbras would already have studied) and from the observation of Fortinbras's own spies. Where had Hamlet been, and what had he done, during that spell of time unaccounted for? Had he not, surely, been occupied in organising a military coup against Claudius? And if so, was there some operation still in motion, some legacy of peril undistracted by the prince's death, waiting out there, in the obscurity of the winter's cold and darkness, for the right moment to strike?

The night was far gone, the chamber in which they sat

achingly cold, its corners cluttered with shadows. Fortinbras turned over the last of the papers, and quickly
reviewed them again, holding each in turn up to the light
of the candle.

The first was a letter Hamlet had sent to Horatio from
an unspecified location:

Prince Hamlet to Horatio
April, 1050

My loving friend Horatio –

You will perceive to hear so soon from your loving
prince that the King's intentions for me go not unim-
peded. Nor will it surprise you to know, in the interim, of
a plot laid against my proper life.

We were embarked, bearing full sail for England. My
loving companions, Rosincrance and Gilderstone, their
courages fortified by draughts of Rhenish, snored like the
seven sleepers. I had no rest; there was a kind of fighting
in my heart that would not let me sleep. My sea-gown
scarfed about me against the bitter cold, I walked the
decks and held some little converse with the mariners.
They are good fellows, who knew nothing of our sovereign master's good intentions. Angered beyond words
against this king, I rashly resolved me to penetrate his
plot. But rashness be praised, for by indiscretion did I
pierce through my schoolfellows' discreet conspiracy.

In the darkness I groped among their belongings and
found what I was looking for. Withdrawing again to my
own cabin, I examined the commission to England and
made so bold – my fear causing me to forget my manners
– to break the seal. O Horatio, what a royal knavery found
I there! An exact command to the King of England, supported by strong reasons importing the safety of both

Denmark and England too, that without hesitation – no, not even time to hone the axe – his highness should have my head struck from my shoulders.

Thus like to find myself fast in a net of villainies, I planned my escape. I sat down and wrote a new commission – using all my forgotten skills of penmanship, providentially remembered – containing an earnest conjuration from our King to his loving cousin of England to put the bearers to immediate death, allowing them not even a moment for a last confession. The ruse could not have been put into such good effect, had I not always carried within my purse my father's signet, the exact model of the Danish seal. I folded and sealed the paper so none could distinguish it from th'other, and placed it where 'twas found. What forethought urged me then to play my own secretary, and to take a copy, I know not. I could ill spare the leisure to do't. But here it is, together with the royal command it supplanted. Read them both, and tell me honestly which has the more engaging style?

I had hoped to witness this fine conclusion to my companions' undertaking. But my safety was to be re-assured by other means: truly there's a divinity that shapes our ends, rough hew them how we may. Ere we were two days old at sea, a pirate of very warlike appointment gave us chase. Finding ourselves too slow of sail, we put on a compelled valour. In the grapple, I boarded them: on the instant they got clear of our ship, so I alone became their prisoner. They have dealt with me like thieves of mercy, but they knew what they did. I am to do a good turn for them. When thou shalt have overlooked this, give these fellows some means to the King: they have a letter for him. Then repair thou to me with as much haste as thou wouldst flee death. These good fellows will bring thee

where I am. Rosincrance and Gilderstone hold their
course for England. Farewell.

He that thou knowest thine,

HAMLET

The second was an official commission written by
Claudius to Cnud of England, and carried by Rosincrance
and Gilderstone, which Hamlet had seized from his sleeping companions.

Claudius of Denmark to Cnud of England
April, 1050

*Claudius King of Denmark by the might of this seal requires
from all his subjects and those of his tributary King Cnud of
England free and safe passage to his loyal commissioners Rosincrance and Gilderstone and their companions through all the
realms of Denmark and England. Let none be so bold as to touch
the King's messengers. This our great seal is to be broken by
none save our loving cousin and liege-man Cnud of England –*

To Cnud, our loyal kinsman and liege-man of
England, from your loving cousin and liege-lord Claudius
of Denmark, greetings.

For the payment of Danegeld being iii ships of treasure and slaves received this two months past, much
thanks.

For the matter of protection against pirates harrying
your eastern shores, we have referred this to Hakon, commander of our western ports. Hakon will assess the situation and report to us. Take all measures meantime
within your powers to repel such outlaws.

Let us now to a matter of greater moment, which near
concerns both our crowns. It is known to your royal self
that unrest and seditious mutinies have plagued us here
in Denmark. Though none could dispute our title, being

King Harald's natural son; and though our election by
the *Thing* was in full and open session approved; there
are not wanting in Denmark unruly subjects ready to
murmur against our rule. Treacherous lords there are,
who will swear allegiance in word and give defiance in
deed. There are such as speak darkly of the days of my
brother Amled, and complain that nought has gone well
in Denmark since his death.

Among these disloyal conspirators is one whose plots
and inductions touch upon both our states. For we have
it on written evidence, and signed confession, that there
is a well-hatched plot abroad to overthrow both ourself
and you, and plant another in both our thrones. These
malefactors affirm that England, late scarred by the
Danish sword, should be a fief of our Danish crown, and
that one king should rule in both our lands. Where we
ourself, notwithstanding our right of conquest, have
received your free allegiance, and generously offered our
protection to your shores, those who would depose us
demand your enforced submission, as they plot our
enforced overthrow.

Of this plot the wicked agent and instrument is, to my
great shame and remorse, none other than mine own
nephew, son to my late dear brother, the Prince Hamlet.
If further proof of his guilt be required, his fame and reputation being so widely known and well regarded, both
for his own sake and for the great deeds of his noble
father, let me confide to you that he has within these last
few hours proven himself, here within our own court, an
instrument of brutal murder, having savagely stabbed to
death, in his mother's own chamber, one well-known to
yourself as a trusty emissary and ambassador, my dear
friend and chief counsellor, Polonius. Though Hamlet
excuse his action with flimsy pretexts, that he thought

the old man an intruder or spy, both his guilt and his malice are by this one vile deed abundantly manifested.

We have of our love and mutual interest provided explanations full and frank, where our power alone might have commanded. For the greater health and safety of both Denmark and England, and for the secure preservation of both our crowns, I bid you without delay or hesitation to put my rebellious nephew to immediate execution. Since he is much loved of the people for his father's sake, there is too much danger in dispatching him here. By this deed you shall renew again that love and kindness you have been wont to receive ever from your loving lord and kinsman

DENMARK

The third was Hamlet's own forged substitute, enclosed within the letter to Horatio:

Claudius of Denmark to Cnud of England

Claudius King of Denmark by the might of this seal requires from all his subjects and those of his tributary King Cnud of England free and safe passage to his loyal commissioners Rosincrance and Guildensterne and their companions through all the realms of Denmark and England. Let none be so bold as to touch the King's messengers. This our great seal is to be broken by none save our loving cousin and liege-man Cnud of England.

To Cnud, my noble cousin and liege-man, King of all England, defender of the faith, rock of the Holy Church, friend to the poor, protector of the weak, in love and friendship from your liege-lord Claudius of Denmark, greetings.

My lord, as near as is your love to the heart of Denmark, so close is the amity between our two states.

Whenever did the world show two such kings, of like authority and sway, yet co-existing in such sweet love and affection between their powers? For the late passage of arms between us, it is now as a forgotten dream. This hand with which I write could as lief be raised in harm against our own life, as Denmark could wish any hurt to fall on England.

Dear cousin, as England is our faithful tributary, so love between us should flourish like a palm tree. We receive your fee, so lovingly and freely paid, not as a forced exaction, but as a gift that graces both giver and receiver.

That peace may still her wheaten garland wear, and bind with love our mutual amities, we crave one boon of our fair cousin England. It is well known to your majesty that rebellious subjects trouble us here in Denmark, as disloyal brigands trouble your own shores. As those pirates have come to fear the might of Denmark, so let our unruly subjects quake in terror at the power of England. Those who bear this commission to you are among the most wicked and disloyal of all my subjects. But yesternight they were here in our own court the occasion of a most heinous murder, the slaying of my own chief counsellor, the good old Polonius, whom you knew well. Though they have with their practis'd cunning concealed their crime, yet are they guilty before the very eye of heaven itself.

Now, that we might better show our mutual power, and command free awe from all our subjects, strike me these villains' heads from off their shoulders.

Our nephew Hamlet, though their schoolfriend from younger days, is innocent of these inductions, and we pray you to afford him your protection. As you show my enemies no mercy, so you will endear to yourself, in new-renewed love, your dear liege-lord and kinsman,

DANMARK

Lastly Fortinbras placed on top of the papers a letter he had found, ragged and stained with travel, among Claudius' state papers:

**Prince Hamlet to King Claudius
May, 1050**

High and mighty –
    You shall know that I am set naked on your kingdom. Tomorrow I shall beg leave to see your kingly eyes; when I shall (first asking your pardon thereunto) recount the occasion of my sudden, and most strange, return. I am, my lord, your loving nephew,

HAMLET

'Are you certain – quite certain – that there is nothing else?'

For some time Fortinbras held Horatio's gaze with his melancholy eyes, intense, attentive, but barely interested in the answer to his own crude interrogator's question, his mind already remote from the trivial point, patiently searching past and future for solutions to the larger problems that formed, fragmented and reformed in his punctilious politician's brain.

He looked down at the letters spread across the table, thin sheets of parchment, thickly written over in close cursive script that flickered in the yellow candle light, alternately yielding and obscuring meaning. Thoughtfully, Fortinbras tapped the papers with the ivory hilt of a small dagger, as if attempting to stabilise their meanings.

He lifted each in turn and examined it: looking at the creases where the letters had been folded; seeking circumstantial evidence of what these writings might have been capable of saying to their recipients, their writers, and to a reader like himself, a third party outside the intended chain of communication.

Horatio, seated on the other side of the table, shook his head. He had carefully selected the documents to form the kind of record, a mixture of public and private testimonies, that Fortinbras would imagine him likely to have kept. Though the process of selection had been deliberate, for Horatio wished to control as tightly as he could the parameters of Fortinbras's knowledge, it gave him some satisfaction to render to Hamlet's successor evidence of the truth concerning the late prince's extraordinary life, and tragic death. Fortinbras would now know the true nature of Claudius's treachery, and the subterfuge of his attempt to have Hamlet killed; the bold and resourceful improvisation effected by the prince in discovering the king's commission, and switching the letters; and perhaps most of all, Hamlet's disarming surrender to Claudius's authority, alone and with no military backing. It was as if he had deliberately provided his uncle with an opportunity of making peace and of laying the past to rest. Everything that had passed between them could have remained unspoken, Hamlet's escape from Claudius's plot providing an opportunity for a reciprocal calling of quits. Except, of course, for the one intractable fact, which Claudius could not know but would always suspect, that Hamlet knew the manner of his father's death. Under the shadow of such suspicion, Claudius could never rest easy in his bed, as long as Hamlet lived, inflamed by that corrosive knowledge, to brood over injury, and to contemplate revenge.

Fortinbras himself would never have considered attempting such a high-risk strategy, and was probably wondering at Hamlet's naiveté in returning, unfriended, to a Denmark that could contain nothing for him but danger. Perhaps he was after all mad, as they said, despite all the evidence to the contrary contained in these papers. Or perhaps he had always remained the fastidious scholar who simply understood nothing of the harsh world of politics and war.

But that was no madman, who had so ably escaped from the entanglements of Claudius's plot. Nor was it any idle intellectual who had thrown in his lot with the pirates, successfully persuaded them to assist him, and sent Rosincrance and Gilderstone to their deaths. Perhaps Hamlet had in actuality been much cleverer than his mighty opposite; and had Laertes not been set on to destroy him, who knows what kind of negotiated truce may have been struck up between the wronged but pragmatic prince, and the suspicious but prudent uncle?

To Horatio's observation, Fortinbras's deepest curiosity seemed compelled by what these letters told him about the story of Hamlet, since he read over their contents carefully more than once. Was he fascinated by the life of the man of whose death, Laertes being his instrument, he had been the agent and prime mover? A murderer often, they say, continues to take an interest in the life of his victim.

Was he considering whether or not he had misjudged

Hamlet, and whether or not such misjudgement had caused him to let slip an opportunity? For surely, in the light of these disclosures, Hamlet would have eagerly joined in an attempt to overthrow Claudius, and a Denmark governed by its own king, that king resting under so deep an obligation to his neighbour, might have been a stronger ally of Norway than a Denmark subjugated to the Norwegian sword.

Or perhaps Fortinbras was wondering whether Hamlet had really acted his part, like some harlotry player. Perhaps he had wished to display the idiosyncracy of behaviour that would seem natural in a lunatic; or to show to the world the impracticality of an unwordly scholar. If he had, then the prince must indeed have left some secret legacy far more threatening to Fortinbras's newly acquired power than the prince's evident qualities of honour and courage, which distinguished the story of his life, and were transparently inscribed in his writings.

He knows, thought Horatio, that I am keeping something back, but he does not know what it is. He cares less about the disloyalty of my reticence, than about the possible danger that might lie in an unrevealed fact, motive or intention. He thinks it must be of some importance to make it worth concealing, but he speculates that it may be some secret he has already guessed, or some piece of mere intelligence he has already acquired from another source. I am sure he cannot know, though he may well suspect, that I know of his correspondence with Laertes.

Despite all the reasons that rendered them enemies, Horatio was impressed by Fortinbras, whose personality and presence were so different from the almost legendary figure of popular report. Scholars like his late prince Hamlet had mocked Fortinbras as an amusing anachronism, a vestigial survival from a remote antiquity. But this Fortinbras was no young adventurer thirsting for heroic deeds and knightly honour but a man of large intelligence, ruthless determination and a passionate conviction of destiny. A man who would be king, and who had already, Horatio guessed, weighed the keen delights of assured power against the haunting anxiety and melancholy resignation that would eventually disturb his rest, and blight his old age.

Fortinbras shivered slightly, rubbing a hand over his cropped skull, for he was shorn in the Norman fashion, and round his black stubble of beard, in an uncharacteristic gesture of tiredness. There was no fire in the draughty chamber where they sat, but neither would make any concession to the cold, other than to shrug himself more deeply into his heavy cloak. Horatio was accustomed to long vigils in monastic cells, weeks of frosty sea travel and, although no soldier, long night-watches on chilly battlements, waiting (in that strange time he recalled as the true beginning of this stranger story) for an apparition that would freeze the blood, and chill the spirit, more icily than any cold of the body.

Fortinbras exuded that soldierly insouciance about place that went with rough temporary bivouacs and hastily constructed command centres; but there was also in him, Horatio thought, something of the saint, some curiosity to mortify the flesh experimentally in order to provoke new initiatives of mind and spirit. How unlike the soft, sensual, pampered flesh of the late King Claudius was this chaste purity of will, in an efficient, ascetic body! If anything, Horatio thought, Fortinbras was more akin to that other son of a slaughtered father, Hamlet, the prince whose lost birthright Fortinbras had fortuitously found himself in a position to seize. For where Hamlet, the cynical idealist, had been shaped by his destiny into an impractical philosopher with a surprising capacity for action, Fortinbras, the machiavellian intellectual, was a dedicated soldier and politician with an equally remarkable propensity for thought. That combination of characteristics made him a formidable opponent in the dangerous game Horatio had elected to play.

'Good night, my friend', said Fortinbras, with a gesture of dismissal. 'Tomorrow the Council meets to determine succession. I will need you' – he pointed with his dagger and elaborated the gesture with the thinnest of smiles – 'to have all your wits about you'

As Horatio walked wearily back to his sleeping place in the hall, where the king's bodyguard noisily snored, he thought, with genuine admiration, of the king to whom he had offered such a perilous conditional service. A king who would one day, almost certainly, have cause to curse his name; a king who might well ultimately attain to the satisfaction of subscribing it to a death warrant.

Horatio had been obliged to give Fortinbras much in return for the relative security he at least temporarily enjoyed. But Horatio had also gained much in this exchange: not only his own safety, but a position of privi-

lege close to the king, one that permitted him certain critical possibilities of knowledge and action. He could easily
have slipped away from Denmark quietly, and re-entered
that life of wandering voluntary exile that was neither
unfamiliar nor even unpleasant to him. All the skills he
possessed were locked in his head: but they were highly
valued and much in demand. Always, somewhere, there
was a lord with children to be taught, a religious community with books to be translated; a king with documents to
be written, problems of statecraft to be pondered, secrets
to be kept.

Horatio settled down to sleep with his head on a
leather satchel that accompanied him wherever he travelled. He had surmised, so far correctly, that the bag
would not be searched unless he were openly arrested, in
which case his days, either in Denmark or on the earth,
would certainly be numbered. Horatio knew that no one
in Helsingor would be capable of deciphering the closely
written sheets carefully sewn into the satchel's lining. By
the time Fortinbras had managed to acquire a translator
capable of reading classical Greek, he would have escaped,
by flight or poison, to the harsh security of the seas or the
final safety of a quiet grave. If translated, the papers,
Greek translations of private letters and papers the
originals of which had been burnt and their ashes cast to
the northern winds, would hint at, but not expound, a
remarkable story. Even they would mean little without
the key that unlocked their secrets, the one missing
thread that completed the tapestry. Horatio knew that he
was the only one who possessed the key, held that thread;

and he would rather take it with him to the ultimate con-
fidentiality of the grave than surrender it to any living
person. He carried the Queen's dying request, as his lord
had carried within him the words of his father's ghost, an
image cherished and haunting, a message of fear and
hope, wonder and terror. Horatio had no idea whether he
would live to execute those commands, uttered with all
the dignity of *articulo mortis**, to find, narrate, and restore.
But he was as certain as any man could be, that no one
else should seize the opportunity, or undertake the quest,
uniquely and imperatively imposed on him. Automatically
he slipped from inside his doublet the locket he had
seized from the Queen's neck, and in the darkness rubbed
his fingers over its decorative surface. Easing his nail into
the seam, he prised the locket open and felt with his
thumb the miniature of King Amled's face. The other half
of the locket, which he knew had contained a portrait of
Claudius, he had found empty.

Horatio muttered a few formal prayers to the Christian
God whose teachings he held in deep respect, and in
whose passionate mystery of sacrifice he partially
believed. But in sleep he dreamed, as he often dreamed, of
ragnr rokr†, the final conflict, the twilight of the gods. He
saw the field of Vigrid, before Valhalla, darkening in the
sun's almost extinguished rays, as the brood of the great
Fenrir, father of wolves, gradually but inevitably devoured
the sun. He saw Odin, resplendent as the sun in his gold

*   last words
†   the end of the world in Scandinavian mythology

helmet plumed with eagles' wings, brandishing the great spear Gungnir, fearlessly confronting the foe. He saw the jaws of Fenrir gape, blasting fire like a furnace; and he saw Odin swallowed easily and whole, his brightness suddenly extinct, as the night devours the day. Frigg, Odin's consort, fainting helplessly from grief and terror, begged the gods to avenge her lord. Then Vidar, son of Odin, flung himself on Fenrir and prised open the huge jaws, holding down the wolf's fangs with his enchanted sandal that no flame could devour, and stabbed downwards into the fiery throat, in revenge for his father piercing the great creature's heart.

Then the darkness of sleep would overwhelm Horatio's mind, as that final darkness closed over Vigrid and buried the *Aesir* *. As a new light began to break over a recreated world, fresh with the softness of dawn, Horatio would wake, his heart brimming with joy of renewal, to the hard grey light of another common day.

To the unsatisfied. Find the boy. Tell my story.

The *scriptorium*†, or secretarial chamber, of Helsingor was normally occupied by a small army of scribes, all busily copying and composing letters, proclamations, minutes, political and state papers of every description. With understandable caution, Fortinbras had ordered them all

---

*   the gods
†   writing workshop

out and Horatio possessed the room alone. Doubtless there were another half-dozen scriveners similarly isolated in other chambers, possibly even working on the same documents, certainly precluded (at least temporarily while Norwegian power was in process of imposition) from any communication with one another.

The room Horatio sat in was high up in a tower of the castle with looped and traceried stone windows affording a wide prospect of the sea. With the winter sun, flat and brassy in a cloudless blue sky, throwing light that twinkled and sparkled on the white-capped waves, and etching into clear visibility the distant cliffs of Sweden, the chamber was a pleasant place to work. Horatio was deriving little pleasure, however, from the work in which he was engaged, which was to write out a transcription of his own record of the Council meeting held at Helsingor that morning, the concluding paragraphs of which were giving him unprecedented trouble in composing. He normally enjoyed the challenge of reducing the vociferous altercations of such meetings to orderly narrative. He invariably took pleasure in the physical processes of writing, loving the smell of ink and the texture of parchment, the satisfying shape of well-formed letters, the graceful perfection of a well-penned page.

He often recalled, as his pen with difficulty etched a smooth linear passage across the uneven texture of parchment, the old riddle describing, in mystifying terms, the construction of a book: how an animal's skin was taken, wetted and folded, scraped smooth with the keen edge of a knife; how a bird's feather greedily swallowed ink, drawing its trajectory across the dark rim of an ink well, then continued on its long, repetitious journey across the page, always leaving behind its black, tell-tale tracks; and how finally the parchment would be bound in tightly fitting skin, and embellished with gleaming gold. As his pen negotiated the various bumpy imperfections of the parchment, he always felt that sense of kinship with the natural world of animal and bird and leaf from which his writing implements derived. In his hand the feather quill still flew across empty space, signing the air with meaning; the patient sheep (sacrificed to a greater work) whose skin provided the parchment, continued, in death as in life, to render obedient service to its human masters; the tree, from whose leaves the ink had been manufactured, now produced ever new, and ever stranger, fruits of the intellect, and flowers of the spirit.

The riddle ended, he remembered, with a pun on the Greek word 'biblia', plural of the noun for 'book', a term which had come to be synonymous with the books of the Bible. Horatio had once come across an illuminated manuscript with an elaborate allegorical emblem showing the Paschal Lamb, Agnus Dei, taking a feather from St John's eagle, dipping its point into the bark of a Tree of Life that was also the Cross of the Passion, and writing across his own white skin, in vivid letters of vermilion blood, the words of the Baptist, the mystery of His own sacrifice: *'Ecce Agnus Dei, qui tollis peccatum mundi.'** There was always some relationship, Horatio reflected, between every word

---

* 'Behold the Lamb of God, who takes away the sins of the world' (John 1.29)

written by men, and the ultimate Word that was said to be in and from the beginning, God, and with God; though most of the time the connection was far beyond the capacity of human intelligence to descry or to prove.

He hoped against hope that the writing he was in process of completing would justly and truthfully serve the memory of his prince and faithfully interpret to the world Hamlet's authentic and original story. That legacy, which he held in trust, had in some inscrutable way become bound up in his mind with ideas of divine providence and memorial sacrament. If he, Horatio, could ultimately find a way, not only of telling, but of completing, that story, then his speech and his writings would ultimately, he believed, fall into conformity (if God existed) with the will of God. It was to be hoped so, he thought grimly, since the words he was about to write would, *prima facie*, fall far short of a truthful account of recent history. They were the record of his own contribution to the debate, and he had by now, considering their importance to Fortinbras, deferred committing them to paper for longer than was prudent or advisable.

As if this point were to be providentially underlined, Horatio heard the door open behind him and stiffened at the sound of the measured, already familiar, tread of his new master. Without turning or looking up, Horatio offered the king a busy, sideways bow of the head and continued with his writing, only pointing to the pile of completed sheets that lay at his right elbow. Fortinbras picked them up, moved over to the window, and leaning on the embrasure, began to peruse the manuscript.

Record of the Great Council of the Danes, Parliamentary Rolls, 1050.I.i–1050.IX.i.

1050.I.i   After the death of King Claudius of noble
memory, the *Thing* met at Helsingore to determine succession. His highness Crown Prince
Fortinbras presided by right of military occu-
pation. Since the sons of King Harald of
blessed memory were now extinct, and
Gerutha[*] the wife of King Claudius died with
her lord, and the son of King Amled was also
perished together with King Claudius, the line
of succession was now at an end. It was the
duty of the *Thing* to decide who should
become king and what family should now
replace that of King Harald in Denmark's
throne. Prince Fortinbras assured the assembly that he would abide by their decision.

1050.II.i   Prince Fortinbras's claim was presented by the
learned advocate Lief Laufiayrsen.

1050.II.ii   "When King Svend, son of Harald, ruled the
Danes, he joined with Anlaf Tryggvassen, King
of Norway, to undertake raids in England.
When King Anlaf fell in battle, the crown of
Norway fell to King Svend. This precedent, my
lords, proves: that in cases where power is
shared between two crowns in alliance, and
one king is killed in battle, then the survivor
is true heir and inheritor to his brother king.
When Prince Fortinbras marched against
Poland, he bore the regal authority of the King

---

[*]   Gertrude

of Norway: he was, my lords, in a legal sense, King.

1050.II.iii "When King Claudius agreed to allow the said Prince Fortinbras free passage through his dominions – as witnessed in this letter of King Claudius's seal – Denmark and Norway did form an alliance. It may plainly be seen, therefore, my noble lords, that when the great King Claudius died, Denmark and Norway were joined in a military alliance.

1050.II.iv "Let me turn now, my lords, to my second proof, that King Claudius did die in battle. First, what is a battle? Second, what is it to die in a battle? if a battle signifies sword drawn against sword, in a fight to the death, with rules of engagement, then the combat between Lord Laertes and Prince Hamlet was a battle. That the combatants may not have intended to do each other harm is not admissible against the argument since, in the event, their mutual slaughter did render the combat a battle. When the Prince Hamlet slew King Claudius, he did so in the course of a battle.

1050.II.v "Therefore, my lords, it is plainly proven: that King Claudius did die in battle, at a time when the crowns of Norway and Denmark were joined in an alliance. Just as, in earlier days, and in like conditions, the crown of Norway did descend rightly to the King of Denmark; so now it is manifestly just that the crown of King Claudius, slain in battle, there being no surviving heirs, should accede to the King of Norway; the said crown to be accepted as regent on behalf of his Norwegian highness King Feng, by the noble Prince Fortinbras".

1050.III.i   The noble Lord Osrik begged leave to address the *Thing*.

1050.III.ii   "My lords, the learned advocate has spoken well, and has proven beyond any doubt that Prince Fortinbras has indeed a most plain and just title to the crown. For has not Norway always been a good friend to Denmark? When a lawless band of pirates gathered a force to attack this kingdom, did not the King of Norway dispatch his own nephew Prince Fortinbras, to protect our borders? And did not this same Fortinbras, at risk to his own life, by bravery and cunning persuade those brigands to march with him against the Polack? So it is proven that Norway, even to its own danger, protected Denmark, and that this protection lay in the person of the noble Prince who now presides over our assembly. Let Denmark now embrace, in earnest, that protection, by accepting Prince Fortinbras as our king. My noble lords, I move the same".

1050.IV.i   The noble Lord Valdemar begged leave to address the *Thing*.

1050.IV.ii   "My noble friend Lord Osrik has the interests of Denmark at heart. A land without a strong king is no land, but a spoil ready to be taken, a prize waiting to be seized. Our warriors no longer know whom they should obey. Some who were sworn to Claudius have lost their leader. Some who supported the cause of young Laertes, when his father was slain by Prince Hamlet, have also lost their general. Some who renounced their allegiance to Claudius, in the hope that young Hamlet would become king, now behold their hoped-for commander shamelessly self-slaughtered.

1050.IV.iii "What future can there be for Denmark without Norway? Civil war, foreign conquest, chaos. What future for a Denmark joined with Norway? Strength, power, stability. I move that the *Thing* offer the crown to Prince Fortinbras".

1050.V.i The noble Lord Thorsten begged leave to address the *Thing*.

1050.V.ii "My lords, as I sit and listen to these courtiers and lawyers, I am truly ashamed to call myself a Dane. They speak of war and conquest, swords and battles. When did any of these water flies see a battle, unless it were a tavern brawl? when did any of them wield a sword, unless it were to fight his way out of a brothel? My lords, I have listened in patience to the ramblings of a learned counsellor and the flattery of courtiers. Since when did the lords of Denmark let matters of such weight be decided by lawyers and lackeys? Danes have ruled in this kingdom for as long as memory can reckon. I pray to Odin that my son should

* defiance

never have to bow his knee to a Norweyan
usurper. I bid defiance to the Norseman and
his army".

1050.V.iii Here the Lord Thorsten placed his sword on
the table in sign of *diffidatio.** The Prince
Fortinbras graciously accepted the pledge, and
promised Lord Thorsten satisfaction.

As Fortinbras reached the end of the sequence of completed leaves, Horatio was ready to hand him the last finished sheet. Fortinbras observed his scribe closely but said
nothing. He continued to read.

1050.VI.i Prince Fortinbras begged the *Thing* to hear the
witness of the Freeman Horatio, loyal servant
of the Danish house.

1050.VI.ii The Freeman Horatio begged leave to address
the *Thing.*

1050.VI.iii "My lords, you know me a humble scholar and
gentleman. I was a servant to Prince Hamlet
and a loyal subject of King Claudius and his
Queen. I witnessed the deaths of the King and
Queen, and the Lord Laertes. I was with Prince
Hamlet when he died. My lords, I can truly
affirm that the late King Claudius being dead,
Prince Hamlet foretold that the election
would light on Prince Fortinbras".

1050.VII.i The Prince Fortinbras requested the *Thing* to
deliberate and give their decision.

1050.VIII.i Here the noble lords and freemen conferred,
and gave their verdict for Prince Fortinbras.
His Highness graciously accepted the crown,
and swore to protect Denmark and her people.

1050.IX.i   All swore allegiance to King Fortinbras, save
the Lord Thorsten, who bidding defiance to
the king, was permitted by privilege of *felag*[*] to
quit the court and ride with his *lith* to Sweden.

'Well done, my servant' said the king, with evident satisfaction. 'That will do perfectly. You write very skilfully, if a little – slowly'.

Horatio risked a sidelong glance at the king's features but could read nothing in them.

'Now' said Fortinbras decisively, 'Make me ten copies of this' and he tossed a scrawled page of writing onto the table. It was now Horatio's turn to preserve his countenance in expressionless immobility, as he read the draft of a royal proclamation.

Proclamation of King Fortinbras of Denmark
July, 1050

By the grace of God and in the name of Fortinbras King of Denmark, the *Thing* of Denmark hereby proclaims as a traitor to king and realm THORSTEN, son of Erik, *jarl* of Jelling.

For that this same Thorsten did, with malice and cunning, conspire against the late King Claudius and sought to encompass his death; and for that in clear disobedience to the will of the *Thing*, Thorsten did oppose the free election of Fortinbras to the crown of Denmark and bid defiance to the lawful king; and for that this Thorsten did flee into Sweden, there to raise an army, sworn to overthrow King Fortinbras and to kill all the lords of the *Thing*; it is hereby proclaimed –

– that Thorsten's life is forfeit to the Danish crown and

[*]   diplomatic immunity

subject to King Fortinbras's pleasure. All subjects of King Fortinbras are commanded to divulge any knowledge of the traitor, to offer him no protection, and to apprehend him if found anywhere in the King's dominions.

Under the King's seal this year of grace 1050 –

DENMARK AND NORWAY

'Very well, my lord,' said Horatio, keeping his eyes still downcast and picking up a new quill.

Forinbras sat sideways for a moment on the edge of the table and leaned towards Horatio. It was as if he felt some compassion for the servant whose loyalty he was testing to such limits.

'My patient friend,' he said, almost kindly. 'You have done good work this day, both for me and for your country. Let this be your last task, then get some sleep. Tomorrow will be another busy day, since the sad obligation falls to us of laying your king, your queen and your prince to rest, where they may sleep peacefully with their fathers.'

'This unwelcome task completed, much more work awaits us. I wish you to lead a delicate embassy to the King of Sweden. Expect to be absent from Denmark for some time. Be ready for departure, on the day following, at first light. Fail me not.'

Horatio bowed his head in assent, and continued writing. Fortinbras studied for a few moments the illegible, absorbed features; then turned and left the chamber.

The boat's black dragon-prow bumped softly against sharp rocks at the foot of the sheer cliff edge. From above, on the promontory, towered the massive mausoleum that provided a final resting-place for the kings of Denmark. No sound beyond a gentle splashing, indistinguishable from the lapping of the tide at the cliff's foot, betrayed the silent, armed men who slipped over the boat's side and into the shallow water. A rope turned around a spur of rock held the craft in place, where it rode gently on the tide, its elegant long neck weaving with a serpentine undulation from side to side, as the warriors mounted a steep path that would take them to the cliff's top, their passage inaudible but for a whispered communication and a soft chink of mail.

A scout lifted his head cautiously above the cliff edge to establish that the tomb was unguarded. The mausoleum, imperially constructed of smooth black marble, rose above them into the faint moonlight. The heavy iron gates, left unlocked, yielded easily to their levering spears, and the tomb of Denmark's kings once again opened its ponderous jaws.

There in the cold dry darkness, fitfully illuminated by guttering yellow candles, lay Denmark's imperial dead, each corpse tightly sheathed in its linen shroud. There lay Claudius, the queen beside him; and beyond them, interred alone, was the long figure of old King Amled, surrounded by his steel arms and armour, gleaming gold grave goods resting on his breast. In stiff isolation he lay apart, as if in aversion from the proximity of the brother who had murdered him and stolen his queen, the widow who had betrayed her husband.

The Danes wasted little time in contemplating the dead, but executed their task with efficient alacrity, lifting the bier on which rested the body of Prince Hamlet and swiftly conveying it from the tomb. Strong warrior arms carefully handed their burden down the cliff face and into the waiting craft. The boat's head pulled round towards the open sea, a taut rope's knot loosened to drop the black sail, which bellied out into the stiff seaward breeze, and propelled the dragon-ship, empty save for its silent occupant, out on the ebbing tide. On the deck lay the corpse of their prince, his shroud uncovered so his face lay open to the heavens, a glint of gold treasure lying on his breast, a sword loosely clasped in the newly broken fingers of his nerveless hand.

On the shoreline a quick spark from a struck flint flared in the blackness, and a sputtering flame rose from an arrowhead soaked in pitch. A bowstring arced back and the blazing missile enacted its bright trajectory across the water. Catching in the cloth of the black sail, its flames soon had hold of the rigging and the dry timbers. Before Fortinbras's guards, alerted by the flickering lights out in the bay, could raise the alarm, the Danes had withdrawn into the silent darkness.

Bear Hamlet like a soldier to the stage. The dragon-ship floated on, bright whirlwinds of fire haloing the hero's sleeping head. For he was likely, had he been put on, to have proved most royal.

His final destination was the warrior's heaven of Valhalla. But in truth no man could tell – neither the crafty counsellor in court, nor the brave hero beneath the blue sky – who, at the last, unloaded that cargo.

Part two

THE DREAMS OF GUDRUN

'In my first dream', said Gudrun, 'I dreamed that on my wrist I found a silver ring: as bright as the moon, and with a sheen like the moonlit surface of the midnight sea. But just when I least expected it, the ring slipped from my hand and fell into water. I never saw it again. What I had lost seemed more than the value of the ornament, or the beauty of a lovely thing. It was more like the loss of a first love. When I awoke, my face was wet with the tears I wept for the loss of my silver ring'.

FROM THE LAXDAELA SAGA

1

Near Helsingor

May 1050

Pendant branches of willow swept downwards to the mountain stream that flowed, swift and translucent, through a deep rocky cleft and over clean white boulders. Peering down through the glassy green swell she could just glimpse white faces, staring up at her. There they were, re-enacting their ceremony of innocence, the cold drowned maids.

The opposite bank was starred with wild flowers, white daisies, black-eyed crow-flowers, blossoming nettles. Phallic buds dangled limply: dead men's fingers. These she desired: to feel their soft flaccidity stiffen against her white hands. She grasped a branch of willow and leaned across, stretching to reach the long purples. With a sharp crack the envious sliver broke, and cascaded her softly, with a cream of foam, into the icy brook.

She sank straight down, her skirt blooming around her. Now she could clearly see the river-maidens, their pale faces haloed with floating green weeds, and now she could clearly hear their sad, sweet song. From below a faint yellow glimmer woke in the depths: the Nibelung's gold. She stretched her long white hands towards her dead sisters.

Feeling the change of pressure, the baby in her womb kicked. From the darkness of his warm living sea, he felt his mother seeking the cold waters of death, and kicked violently against her in instinctive resistance.

Breaking the surface, she leaned back, entrusting her body to the white arms of the water-maidens, who bore her up and steered her, gently but swiftly, downstream. The child rested softly in the dark inland lake of her belly. She took up the maidens' song, a sweet and plaintive lay, melancholy with the sadness of dying love.

> He is dead and gone, lady,
> He is dead and gone.
> At his head a grass-green turf,
> At his heels a stone.

She floated on, mermaid-like, as if incapable of comprehending her own peril. Slowly her sisters let her sink, till the waters covered her fair round belly and her lovely face.

> And will he not come again?
> And will he not come again?
> No, no, he is dead ...

Too much of water hast thou, poor Ofelia. Goodnight ladies; goodnight sweet ladies. Goodnight. Goodnight.

2
Helsingor

June 1049

'**M**y lord Polonius? Pray you, sir, a few moments of your in*valuable* time'.

Polonius involuntarily stiffened at the sound of the familiar voice: so relaxed and arrogant, so superior in its nuanced drawl. But it was nonetheless with a servile bow, and an unctuous tone of civility, 'At your service, my Lord Hamlet', that he turned to the young prince and waited, with apparent attentiveness, to hear what he had to ask.

Hamlet had no illusions as to Polonius's feelings towards him. Yet he never let slip any opportunity of irritating the old counsellor, by continual small reminders of the power he held, both as Amled's son, the Prince of Denmark, and as the future king, over his father's chief minister. Polonius had little hope of his career surviving into another reign: the gap between his generation and that of young men like the prince, and his own son, Laertes, had widened appreciably compared to the narrow fault-line that had, in previous generations, separated father from son. And after all it was their own doing, this production of an arrogant and condescending generation. It had been the explicit policy of men like himself, and the king's brother, Claudius, to steer the culture of court and government away from the primitive, fighting, drinking and whoring ambience of King Harald's household.

But at least, he considered with some resentment, the sons of Harald, and their retainers, had served their time in the hard school of war. If they had not all won heroic reputations like Svend and Amled, at least they partici-pated in the management of battle. At least they had endured the hardships of the field and tolerated the rough camaraderie of the camp. And it was out of that practical experience that men like Claudius and himself had formed the vision of a new Denmark: a civil state, capable of both aggression and defence, but not based on the exigencies of continual destructive and self-destructive action. A Denmark whose leaders knew from experience the heavy cost of war, and were also clever enough to know when to fight, when the fighting had to stop, and when it was more intelligent to avoid fighting altogether.

One of their rewards was to be treated with contempt by the younger generation; regarded as caterpillars of the commonwealth, men of inaction who had sold Denmark's heroic past for dishonourable treaties. Yet the irony was, young men like Hamlet and Laertes had been kept well clear of the smoke of battle. They had been educated in the new humanist programme favoured by the emergent European monarchies as the appropriate way to train the princes of the future. True, they had all learned, in the tilt-yard, the arts of chivalry and the skills of combat; they could all dress brilliantly in gold and silver armour and coloured plumes; they could all joust bravely for a lady's favour. But it was all play-acting, innocuous juvenile fun. Yet it was from their success in such exhibitions, war games conducted in conditions of peacetime leisure, that the gilded youth of Denmark formed their nostalgia for the heroic days of Denmark's past glories. It was from their success in such displays that they derived their contempt for the men they saw as government bureaucrats, elderly parasites of the court.

No one exuded this air of polite condescension so strongly as Hamlet. Polonius had no choice, the source of his irritation being none other than the king's only son, and the heir apparent, but to swallow his pride and endure a persistent, almost intangible stream of mockery. One of Hamlet's strategies for baiting Polonius was to assume an exaggerated politeness, an elaborate tone of high courtesy. Others seemed to find it wickedly clever and amusing. Polonius could see in it nothing clever, and was sure that whatever humour was afforded, was at his own expense.

Hamlet had stopped the old man in a corridor as he hastened towards the Great Hall on some errand and addressed him in exactly such a tone.

'My felicitations to you, my most honourable lord, and to your son the noble Laertes. But,' he continued, linking his arm familiarly with Polonius', and conducting him in a leisurely stroll on the route he had been following, 'it was of your *daughter*, the Lady Ofelia, that I wished to speak. I was struck, my lord, I must tell you – I know no other way of putting it – struck, on observing your fair daughter yesterday in court, by her beauty and accomplishments. But where have you been hiding this jewel, my lord? Locked in some dusty old treasure-chest, like a miser hiding his wealth from the prying gaze of thieves and robbers? I trust you have no fears that any should try to steal your daughter from you, here in my father's well-guarded castle? Such brightness of face, such riches of figure should surely be brought into the light. When, my lord Polonius, may we hope to see the fair Ofelia again?'

'So', thought Polonius, covering his suspicion with an expression of bland obedience, 'this is his highness' new jape. I might have expected it. It would surprise me nothing if this young popinjay had not cooked up some practical joke with his friend, my vagabond son. Yes, they have been very thick of late, whispering and giggling like schoolboys, egging one another on to such daring exploits as this, whate'er it may be: to fool an old man, perhaps – or to break a poor maiden's heart'.

Overtly he bowed again to his young sovereign, in recognition of the compliment to his daughter.

'My lord Hamlet knows, of course, that my daughter is yet young: and indeed was, this day past, making her first appearance in court. I am pleased to hear that your highness acknowledges her debut with undeserved praise. I will, sir, with your gracious permission, have words with the maid, and convey to her your kind and most complimentary attentions. And if you wish, I will seek to prevail upon her to make her next appearance as soon as may be desired.'

Hamlet raised a sardonic eyebrow. Was Polonius admitting the limitations of his paternal control? The old man hastened to explain his reservations. Having grown up without a mother's guiding hand (Polonius' wife having died in delivering her), habitually in the care first of nursemaids, then of governesses and tutors, his daughter had developed a certain strength of character, and was often deemed independent of mind, and capable of displaying some wilfulness, and stubborness of temper.

'These traits are, as my lord will not need reminding, though venial in one of tender years, less tolerable, even odious in a young lady of fashion and society. But rest assured, that whatever a loving father, careful of his children's welfare, can do, that my lord may take assurance will be done, so to effect your gracious and most sovereign wishes'.

And with a parting bow, Polonius turned and left Hamlet standing in the centre of the corridor, hands clasped behind him, deep in absorbed meditation. He hardly noticed the old man take his departure. He was oblivious to a group of courtiers who greeted him respectfully, awkwardly skirted the wall of the corridor to avoid his black-clad, obstructive form, then in turn passed on towards the hall, conferring in excited whispers. What ailed the prince? From what source derived this unusual air of distraction?

Polonius had guessed correctly that Hamlet's accosting him had its origin in a childish prank. It was indeed the case that Laertes had put Hamlet up to this initiative. Otherwise Hamlet would not even have recognised

Ofelia's features among the crowd of equally young and similarly pretty faces. His memory of her was of a tomboy of a girl, who fought with her brother, and who had then disappeared, as all girls did at the age of puberty, into a long sequestration from all public contact, emerging when she reached the age considered appropriate to social reintegration.

This 'meat-market', as the young men satirically termed it, was the ancestor of later rituals of initiation whereby young women were openly declared 'out'. Here they were declared full members of society, fair game for the matrimonial aspirations or predatory lusts of men on the look-out for wives, concubines or mistresses. Though little more than children, overnight they became marriageable, seducible, beddable. Ofelia's companions were all young women being presented for the first time, shyly huddled together before the brash, insulting gaze of the male courtiers. All looked identically scrubbed and fresh, hair scraped back to emphasise their soft, clear skin; mouths smeared with vermilion to give a fullness not yet conferred by maturity; eyes sharply drawn round with charcoal to emphasise their size, brilliance and colour. All wore long white dresses, suggesting the purity of maidenhood, a blank *tabula rasa* on which men might hope to set their proprietary imprint. All bore chaplets of white flowers bound around their brows. Lambs to the slaughter: sacrificial victims of some general immolation.

Admittedly, once Laertes had pointed out to Hamlet the face of his sister, the prince found himself in little need of persuasion to concede that Ofelia certainly stood out from the crowd. Her face was whiter, and her features more clearly marked; her full, slightly protuberant eyes needed no underlying colour to emphasise their lucid, sea-green beauty. And was it only Hamlet's fancy, piqued to curiosity by Laertes' encouragement, or did Ofelia seem different from the others? With her taller stature and more developed frame, her small sharp breasts pushing at the tightness of her bodice, her body suggested with every motion some promise of voluptuousness, some erotic capability beyond her years.

Now Polonius had intimated that Ofelia was, in addition to the physical impression she had made on Hamlet, also a girl of intelligence and spirit, his interest in her was intensified. As he stood there in the draughty stone corridor, he found his imagination suddenly occupied with the image of her face, isolated from the crowd of girls who seemed to shrink into the background as inferior creatures of some other element. Now in his mind's eye he could see, as he had not seen when initially observing her, how her face exuded character as well as beauty: how her green eyes were alight with intelligence as well as loveliness; how her mouth inscribed in its haughty lines an expression of self-sufficiency as well as a rich promise of erotic sensation.

For the first time in his life Hamlet found himself adrift, loose from his moorings, rocked by gentle but inexorable currents. He shivered slightly, becoming aware at the same time of the absurdity of his position, standing in the thoroughfare, so lost in thought as to be oblivious of his surroundings. What was happening to him? Prince

Hamlet, an object of curious attention, even perhaps of some gentle mockery? The observed of all observers, quite, quite down.

'In my second dream', said Gudrun, 'I had another arm-ring, this time fashioned of pure gold. The bright yellow thing seemed a compensation for the loss of my silver ring. I believed that this ring would be faithful to me, and would not betray me as the other did.

'Then in my dream I seemed to stumble, and putting out my hand to save myself, my gold ring struck on a stone and shattered in pieces. To my horror I saw that each piece was bleeding, as if it were torn flesh. I looked closely at the fragments, and saw that the gold had been full of flaws. It was not worth mourning; and yet my mind was full of sadness. It seemed to me that if I had taken better care of the ring, I might have kept it unbroken. The loss of this ring was like the loss of a loved husband. So when I woke, my face was wet with the tears I wept for the breaking of my golden ring.'

FROM THE LAXDAELA SAGA

Now he was alone with Ofelia, Hamlet's customary eloquence of speech and fertility of wit had deserted him.
Her appearance in court had proved something of a
surprise, since on the day following his request to Polonius,
the old counsellor had approached him with an elaborate
agenda of pretexts to excuse his daughter's failure to
reappear.

'May I, my lord, on behalf of my dear daughter, convey
to you my sincere regrets that an indisposition prevented
Ofelia yester-noon from appearing in court. She is now
recovered in health, and it is my hope that ere long you
will see her in company. I have strongly urged my daughter, at your request, to comply with your highness' will.
But if my dear lord will not be angered by a loyal servant's
counsel in these delicate matters, may I presume with a
word of advice? Young women in these days are, as your
lordship well knows, schooled and learned as though they
were young men. My daughter lacks nothing in obedience.
Yet in faith to win her consent in this, my lord could do no
better than to address his wishes to the lady Ofelia in her
own person. If her demeanour has displeased you, let me
plead for her that she is very young, and unused to society.
The attentions of so gracious a prince will, I doubt nothing, bring her forward as her place and breeding require'.

Though in appearance unmoved by Polonius's repre-
sentations, acknowledging them only with a polite bow,
Hamlet had been inwardly shocked at his own disappointment; then almost relieved that the meeting he had antic-

ipated with mingled excitement and fear was not to take place. He took Ofelia's absence, together with Polonius's elaborate apology, to constitute a refusal. Initially this filled him with a corrosive disenchantment, that was soon followed by an emotion of pique, which allowed him to settle into a more familiar pose of wounded dignity. Who among his father's subjects had the temerity to thwart his sovereign desire?

Now, the very next day as he entered the hall, wearing his habitual air of bored indifference, suddenly she was there, waiting for him. She immediately assumed the advantage, curtseying before him with what might have been exaggerated docility, then waiting (with obvious enjoyment of his discomfiture) for some response to her greeting. Hamlet had blushed, stammered and looked around him for any male companions who might help to extricate him from this embarrassment.

Ofelia had chosen both her moment and her position, he had to admit, with consummate skill. If this was to be another episode in some battle of the sexes, she was already ahead of him in the game. He sat with her in one of the curtained recesses set aside for private audiences. Surrounded by thickly embroidered hangings that billowed gently, with a soft erotic undulation, in the light summer breeze that entered through a slit of window set in the deep stone wall, his composure gradually returned. He began to enjoy the society of one who, having established a position of advantage, seemed more than willing to make his acquaintance.

He began awkwardly, conscious of the amused

expression in her eyes, though her face spoke only polite attention.

'My lady, forgive my familiarity. From my friendship with your brother Laertes I feel I already know you well. Laertes informs me that you have a disposition more inclined to learning and devotions than to worldly pleasures, and that you prefer to shun the press of courtly society. 'Tis becoming modesty in a young woman. But so fair a face as yours should not be kept hidden from appreciative eyes. Even here in my father's court, there are such as take greater pleasure in learning and culture than in feasting and drinking. I bid you show mercy to them, my sweet lady, and grant them the benefit of your society. I have, as my lady knows, had words with your dear father on this matter; and though, as your prince, I might command, I do, being in affection but your humble servant, only entreat you to permit me a better acquaintance'.

Hamlet felt again the sense of disorientation that left him unsure of his words. He was distracted by Ofelia's physical presence, by her perfume, by the white curves of her breasts showing clearly through the thin muslin of her gown. Ofelia's lips had imperceptibly tightened at the word 'command' and her eyes glazed over with momentary hostility. She sat upright, drawing slightly away from him, and replied in a tone of measured courtesy:

'I am honoured to receive your highness' kindly words of commendation. But I fear that the object of your gracious praise is of less value than the adulation. That my face is considered fair, is praise to my mother, who gave it me. If my mind be educated, let the quality be ascribed to my father who taught me. As for modesty – well, I would wish the gift of that virtue to my dear brother. He might show more of it in his own speech and behaviour, before he seeks to protect his sister's honour.'

Seeing disappointment cloud his features, Ofelia looked frankly into Hamlet's eyes and laid a confiding hand on one of his. 'My lord, let us understand one another. You know there are many ladies in your father's court, of far greater beauty, and without the trammels of modesty to curb their forwardness. I pray you, my good lord, seek the company of such as these, and let me find a quiet place of stillness and peace fitting a loyal – and virtuous – subject.'

Hamlet returned her gaze in some perplexity. His interest in what she had to say made him almost forget her femininity, and as he warmed to the argument he began to speak to her almost as if she had been a man:

'You speak truly when you praise the virtue of modesty in women. Such a disposition graces a lady, inclines her from idle pleasure, fixes her mind on truth and learning. But it befits not that she withdraw herself from the society of such as would be more than glad to taste of her learning, and to receive from her piety the blessings of sweet grace. You do mistake me quite should you believe me eager for the company of immodest women, whose free manners pass for wit, and whose unchaste deeds are praised as honourable by the swinish multitude. No, my lady, it is not in these terms that I address you. You must know me, from your brother and your father, as a man more devoted to philosophy than pleasure, and as one whose chief love is private conversation with the wise and learned. I beseech you, in the name of the love I bear Laertes, and my father's friendship to the good Polonius, to bear yourself more openly in court, that you may receive the admiration due to you from your prince and servant.'

Ofelia's amused smile had returned, and her resistance faded away, as if disarmed by the prince's protestations.

'Perhaps, my lord, I do not explain myself well. My dear brother may have borne honest witness to my character. But if he has not, I would not wish your lordship to fall under the illusion that modesty of demeanour, and a disinclination to frivolity, betoken in a maid either weakness, silliness or a readiness to succumb easily to the promptings of others – even such as are greater than themselves. Your lordship knows himself to be my prince, son to my king, and one day my king in your own right and title. As such, I love and honour you as a good subject should. Yet my own virtue as a maid, and the dignity of my family, I prize in good earnest as highly as my loyalty to my sovereign.'

Again she took his hand, and earnestly continued: 'If your lordship wishes in truth to know me better, then I pray you to know me as I am: a lady, neither foolish nor fearful; of good family, and a father favoured by the king; a lover of learning, but no ink-stained scholar; a friend to Holy Church, but no pale veiled sister; modest as becomes one of my years and situation, and free of all desire to have my character, even to my advantage, mistook. If my lord wishes better acquaintance with such a one, I am at your service.'

Ofelia stood and extended her hand straight towards Hamlet in a confident, manlike fashion. 'Now we understand one another, let us hereafter be friends. Shall I see you in court tomorrow?'

Hamlet nodded in reply; and she left him, alone in the bower, paralysed into inaction, but acutely aware of the sensation, like a soft humming in his blood, left behind by her now absent, but to his senses still vividly tangible, body, a keen irritant of desire that lingered like an inscrutable perfume.

$$\oplus$$

The noise of the castle gates creaking open, a drumming of horses' hooves, ragged shouts of men and the deep baying of boar hounds, drew her to the window of her chamber.

Ofelia had risen before dawn, fumbling her way around the darkness of her room, with difficulty washing and dressing and brushing her long hair, making as little noise as possible so as not to disturb the maidservant who still slept soundly curled in her blanket.

A point of light was just piercing the eastern darkness, and beginning to dispel the waning light of the stars, as she knelt, fully costumed and jewelled for appearance in the court, at her *prie-dieu*. She fixed her eyes on the black wooden crucifix nailed to the white wall and began threading her way through the beads of her rosary. The noises of an early expedition aroused her curiosity. She leaned across the embrasure and craned her neck downwards to see what was afoot.

A hunting party was noisily leaving the castle. In the dawn light she could make out the shadowy shapes of horses, bunching together as their riders pushed them down the slope into the valley, then stringing out as each mount was forced at a trot up the opposite incline. The great dogs, leashed in pairs, were fairly dragging their keepers behind them to keep pace with the riders and uttering continuously a resonant baying of pursuit. She could hardly see the riders, mantled in their bristling furs, who seemed to grow centaur-like out of the backs of their horses. The rays of the rising sun flashed intermittently on a metal stirrup, a steel hoof, the point of a spear. From the raw and ragged edge audible in their voices, the men were probably still drunk from the previous night's carouse.

Ofelia pressed her lips together in disdain, turned from the window and knelt again to resume her interrupted devotions.

At mid-morning, when the court began to assemble in expectation of the king's first appearance of the day, she entered the hall. She was dressed brilliantly in the white gown that she knew became her best, fair hair flowing over her shoulders, cheeks rouged with nervous excitement, and looked around for sight of the prince. Hamlet was nowhere to be seen. Normally it was his custom to be up betimes, and to spend the early morning hours, before the throng of courtiers gathered, reading by the fire. Puzzled,

Ofelia strolled with ostentatious nonchalance around the perimeter of the hall. Pausing beside a small group of young men, she overheard from their conversation that a party of gallants, having spent the whole night in drunken revelry, had decided at first light to ride in pursuit of the boar. Just before moving off to distance herself from such boyish dialogue, she heard the name 'Hamlet' mentioned, and gathered, to her indignation, that the prince with whom she had sealed a compact of friendship and agreed to meet that day, was himself a member of the party.

Ofelia marched straight from the hall, ignoring the various courtesies offered to her, and returned to her room. Taking a book from the shelves, she slapped it onto the table and scraped back a chair. Her maid, entering, was told to leave her mistress alone, and retreated as quickly as she had come from that palpable blaze of white, indignant anger.

Ofelia read in silence – or at least stared at the page, for she had no idea what she was reading – as the day wore on, the sun began to decline towards the western hills, and the shadows lengthened across her chamber-floor. Only when she heard uneven hoof beats did she rise and glance from the window to take in the sight of the hunting party returning. The horses were breathing hard and lathered with sweat; the men couching their stained spears, wet and dirty but alight with the triumph of their sport. Two bristling carcasses of boar, hides criss-crossed with streaks of dried blood, were slung across the saddle of one of the horses. Concealing her face in the shadows, she watched the party file towards the gates until she recognised, framed by a black bearskin, the pale face and fair hair of Hamlet. Then she turned on her heel, left the chamber, and walked straight down the stairs towards the central courtyard of the castle.

She met him at the turn of a corridor as he limped wearily from the courtyard where the hunters were dismounting, their friends clustering around to view the kill. Grooms were seizing and unsaddling the horses, servants taking charge of spears, and checking their points and shafts for damage. Young women approached with exaggerated timidity gingerly to finger a yellow tusk or the tough pig-bristle of a boar's hide.

Hamlet, his face white, and marked with shadows of debauchery under the eyes, gave an apologetic smile and leaned as if in exhaustion against a wall.

'Well, my lady. I find I am able to bellow after a boar with the best of my companions; yet my aching bones inform me that I am not after all more suited to the pleasures of the chase than I am to the chasing of pleasures.'

'My lord,' Ofelia began, in a voice of measured fury: 'Today as befitted my duty I complied with your desire: bore myself openly in court, and waited to receive your highness' attentions. What do I find? I am not, as I expected, sealed to my prince in greater friendship and affection, but instead bereft of his companionship, condemned to hear the common prattle of courtly flatterers and to solace my own solitude with memories of your lordship's favour'.

'Pray, my lady,' Hamlet replied, with an uneasy

assumption of politeness, 'Forgive your prince this truant disposition. It is no discontent with your society that drew me from your side. Do not the pleasures of the court sometimes cloy on the sober spirit?'

Ofelia found this impersonal courtesy more insulting than the crudest diatribe. 'You know right well, my lord, that I gave my friendship not easily but freely and with all my heart. For a maid like myself to find a man of like sentiment and reason seemed to me a precious prize, one which I would not willingly part withal. Yet now, when I might in truth hope to expect continuance of that sympathy, my lord instead shuns me, and spends his days hunting with companions unworthy of his grace and princely virtue. My lord, if such is the society you prefer, then you are not what I took you for. Fare you well'.

She began to walk rapidly away but there was something in the tired despair of his voice as he called her, 'Ofelia!' that made her pause and half-turn towards him.

His cheek against the wall, eyes fixed on a spot of flaking white wash on its surface, he spoke in a small dry voice.

'Lady, you do not well understand me. I crave your forgiveness'. After a long pause he seemed to determine with himself the outcome of some irresolution. 'Believe me, Ofelia, that when I begged you to show me the brightness of your countenance, there was no ill will in my intention. I offered you friendship, in all sincerity. At closer quarters, I found that friendship nearer akin to love. To win the heart of a chaste maid by dishonest blandishment is a base proceeding, not worthy a man of honour. Had I offered love, you might have accepted or declined my suit at your pleasure. I offered you the gift of friendship, not then knowing that the cunning little god of passion lurked behind your smile, ready to work his mischief. Now 'tis done, and in sorrow I ask that my gift, now become a mere conjurer's trick to catch unawares a maiden's eyes, be restored to me. I beg you to think better of your prince than he deserves. Fare you well, Ofelia'.

It was now her turn to be left standing alone in the corridor, her eyes gazing at the spot where he had stood, as if his ghost still lingered there, haunting the scene of his renunciation.

PRINCESS KREIMHELD'S DREAM

In her dream Princess Kreimheld thought she had hatched and reared a hawk, wild and magnificent, its plumage beautiful, a fierce untamed light in its golden eye. But as she cast it from her wrist on its first flight, two great eagles swooped and tore it to pieces. The loss of her hawk seemed the bitterest fate that had ever befallen her.

On awakening she sought her mother, Uote, and told her of her dream. 'The falcon you reared', said the wise old woman, 'is a noble knight who will one day become yours. But unless God protects him, he will as soon be wrested away from you'.

'Why speak to me, mother', replied the maiden, 'of a man as my destiny? No warrior's arms will ever embrace me. I will never surrender my beauty to the love of a knight, but will keep it for myself to my dying day. I'll never cry for the love of a hero: no man is worth it'.

'Do not forswear so forcefully, my child', said her mother. 'If you are ever to know true happiness, it will come from a man's love. And if by the grace of God you should win to your love a noble and worthy knight, he himself will protect and foster your beauty'.

FROM THE NIBELUNGENLEID

Ofelia slammed the door of her chamber behind her and, eyes tightly shut, pressed her back against it. She was unable to control a spasm of trembling that shook her body from head to toe. As the tempest of passion subsided, she walked over to her writing desk and sat down, pressing cool fingers against her pulsing temples. Then she snatched up a sheet of parchment, brushed it flat with her hand, caught up a quill, stabbed it into the ink-well, and composed herself to write.

The Lady Ofelia to Prince Hamlet

My lord, I know not what to reply to your words so sweet, your feelings so noble and commendable. But why indeed should you believe your expressions of love unwelcome to my all too open ears? Do I seem so hard of heart as to reject, out of hand, the offer of a true and virtuous love from one in whose arms I would fain die, rather than live a maid? O my lord, I have said too much. To our next meeting, and may it be soon, O soon, my sweetest lord, your devoted

OFELIA

She penned the signature with slow, undulating strokes, as if inscribing into the letters of her name the lineaments of her passion. Then she sanded the letter, brushed off the grains, folded it three times; took a red sealing stick, melted its end in the flame of a candle and dribbled a small circle of molten wax onto the folded edge of the paper. As the wax cooled, she set her signet ring, without removing it from her finger, firmly into the seal. The mingled smells of parchment, ink and singed wax wafted a pungent scent to her nostrils. It occurred to her that she would never forget that scent, and that it would always be associated with this reckless moment of abandonment and self-offering, just as the smell of incense was inseparable to her from the solemn mystery of the Eucharist.

The letter lay folded before her upon the desk. She sat and looked at it for a long time. Then she called her maid, and bid her bring one of the palace messengers to convey a communication to the Lord Hamlet.

As the messenger walked briskly down the flagged corridor, three young men emerged from the shadows of a side turning and silently blocked his path. One of them he recognised as the young Laertes, son to Polonius the second most powerful man in Denmark. With very little sign of any moral indecision, he handed the letter over into Laertes's outstretched hand, took in exchange the proffered coin and made himself scarce.

Laertes looked down at the letter in his hand, lips pursed tightly in an expression of distaste. Checking his thumb as it sought the edge of the seal, he reflected that it had better be delivered to his father intact. He would learn of its contents soon enough.

She sat on the edge of her bed, waiting in agony of uncertainty. He must by now have received it, read it. Perhaps he was held, like her, in an inertia of trepidation. Perhaps he was already regretting the radical indiscretion of his disclosure, and burning her letter in the flame of a candle, or casting its torn leaves into the fire. Perhaps he had already slumped into unconsciousness after his long carnival of debauchery and sport, and her painful vigil would be prolonged until he woke. Perhaps ...

There was a quiet tap at the door. Leaping from the bed, she flung it open to find another servant, holding in his extended hand a sealed letter. At first she thought it was her own missive returned unopened but on closer observation recognised the royal seal. The man hovered as if waiting for a reply but, oblivious to his embarrassment, she closed the door in his face and took the letter back into her chamber.

She tore open the parchment and with difficulty focused her eyes on the page.

Prince Hamlet to the Lady Ofelia
June, 1049

To the celestial, and my soul's idol, the most beautified Ofelia. In that sweet name I name both my sovereign and my tormentor. To plead for her pity, her humble subject begs that she may place thus, in her excellent white bosom, these trifling but heartfelt verses, penned by one whose gift of eloquence comes nowhere near the lofty height of his subject:

> Doubt thou the stars are fire,
>> Doubt that the sun doth move,
> Doubt truth to be a liar,
>> But never doubt I love.

O dear Ofelia, I am ill at these numbers, I have not art to reckon my groans, but that I love thee best, O most best believe it; Adieu.

HAMLET

Leaving the letter on the table, she rose and left the room.

Hamlet lay on his bed half-undressed and through his chamber window watched the sun's last rays touch with melancholy gold the darkening horizon. His man had returned, intimating that the young lady had returned him no reply. In place of the pleasant weariness of physical exhaustion, he began to feel a kind of dwindling enervation in his soul, as if he were suddenly confronted by the ending of his youth, or even by an anticipatory prospect of death itself.

As he drifted off towards sleep, in a waking dream Ofelia appeared before him, standing at the foot of his bed, her face shining like the face of an angel on some mission of annunciation. Opening his eyes, he perceived that in substance, not as a phantom, she was truly there. Then she was in his arms, and he could see nothing but sunlight, as if he had taken the dayspring itself into his bed.

My soul's idol. Her excellent white bosom. That I love thee best, O most best, believe it.

THE DREAMS OF GUDRUN

'In my third dream', said Gudrun, 'I was wearing a beautiful helmet of bright gold, all studded with precious gems. I had never seen the helmet before, but I knew it as my own, as though it were a gift from the gods.

'The day was hot, and the helmet heavy. I could scarcely bear its weight, and felt myself stooping beneath its burden. I did not blame the helmet: it was mine, and I resolved to keep it. Yet although I desired it so, and took such care to preserve it, as I walked by the Hvammsfjord it tumbled from my head, and fell with a splash into the water. The loss of my helmet seemed a greater grief than the loss of my gold and silver rings. It was as if all beauty had gone from the world: my loss was inconsolable, like the loss of life itself. So when I woke from this dream my face was wet with the tears I wept for the loss of my golden helmet'.

FROM THE LAXDAELA SAGA

3
Neaʀ Helsingoʀ

May 1050

A bove, in the inverted mirror of the stream's surface, there was only the sun's broken and refracted image. Then grotesque shapes of men, bent and hooded, rippled into vision. Strong hands seized her shoulders and drew her clumsily, water cascading from the sodden folds of her dress, out from the stream and onto a grassy bank. Twisted roughly onto her side, the water that had burned her throat with such a fierce pleasure of self-annihilation was coughed back out of her. Cold mountain air pierced her lungs and the unwilling heart heaved to beat again.

Before she could realise her new surroundings, she was hoisted from the bank and carried swiftly up a thin track which soon disappeared into the cloistered cool of a forest. Ofelia watched in a dream the bright rays of the sun shatter and re-form between the tops of the high pines. The men who bore her were inscrutably silent, their sandalled shoes scuffing the wood's dry and leafy floor.

Then the steepled bulk of a building loomed above her, grey stone walls, a glimpse of an inverted bell in a tower. She saw the smooth inner stones of a pointed arch and was aware of a dark interior, pierced by coloured light from stained-glass windows. She was laid, gently enough, on a wooden table in a small side-chapel. Her head stretched back and her eyes raised, she could see, upside-down, a figure of the Virgin, baby wrapped protectively in her blue cloak, lifting two fingers in blessing. Votive candles flickered at her feet.

She woke from what seemed a long oblivion to apprehend her surroundings, now curiously thin and unreal. The walls seemed made of paper, the vaulted ceiling about to tear open and admit the bright sun and blue sky. The Holy Mother had conversely become real, her figure standing out from a background of fragile, disintegrating matter, her pitying eyes enlarged to absorb all of Ofelia's distress, her mouth moving in voiceless prayer and benediction. Pray for us now, and at the hour of our death.

'Ofelia'.

The muscles of her neck would not move: her whole body lay paralysed. Only her senses of sight and hearing, unnaturally sharpened, gave her assurance that she was still in the world.

Faces appeared above her: the stern brown features of a man, his head cowled in a black hood; and a woman's face, blurred and unrecognisable, forming into definition – the Queen, her eyes as wide in grief and pity as those of the Madonna.

Though her body seemed as if already discarded, she felt within herself a movement, a quiet stirring as if life were returning, but this time without sadness or pain. The man's face turned towards the Queen and his head shook in a taut, dismissive negative. Gertrude's eyes widened further and shook down irrepressible tears. The man continued to stare at her as if in urgent and imperative demand. Then her eyes closed, and she nodded assent.

Another man's face appeared, holding before Ofelia's eyes a wooden crucifix with the white body of the Saviour twisted in agony across its racking beams. His whispered words meant nothing to her: the Holy Mother, now smiling down on her, knew that she was sorry for her sins, and had already agreed to intercede for her with the Almighty Father. She felt, through her body's insensibility, the soft touch of oil on her hands, her feet and her forehead. It was her own right hand, lifted gently for her by the Queen's long white fingers, that traced across her body the sign of the cross, from head to breast, from shoulder to shoulder. *In nomine patris. Et filii.* The son.

Then with a last pitying look, Gertrude's face disappeared. Ofelia felt, still without pain, another line drawn across her body, again in the shape of the cross: though this seemed more like an incision, a spear-thrust cutting deep into her side; and she heard, just before the final unconsciousness drowned her senses, the loud and indomitable cry of a new life.

Her death was doubtful. Sweets to the sweet: farewell.

THE BIRTH OF VOLSUNG

King Rerir acquired great wealth in war, and took to wife a fair woman for his queen. Long they lived together, but to their mutual sorrow bore no child to receive their inheritance. To the gods they prayed, with heart, soul and mind, that they might be granted the gift of a child.

Odin heard the warrior's prayer, and Freya heeded the petition of the woman. Soon the queen knew that she was with child, and they rejoiced. But her pregnancy was long and heavy, and under its burden she began to grow sick. King Rerir must needs go to the wars, as does any king who hopes to preserve peace in his lands; though it was with a heavy heart that he left his travailing queen behind.

In his absence she pined yet more, and her body grew weaker as the child in her womb waxed in strength. Six long winters passed, and yet she was not brought to bed. Fearing that her own death would slay the unborn child, she called her physicians, and ordered them to cut the child from her. Though they feared to undertake such a deed, more especially in the absence of the king, yet was her passion so peremptory that they dared not disobey. So they cut the child from her body. He was a man child, already before his birth grown greater and stronger than any mortal ever born. To him was given the name Volsung, and he grew to be the greatest of warriors, the most successful in battle, and he ruled over all Hunland in his father's stead.

But the old storytellers also remembered his poor mother, and say that the new born Volsung kissed her tenderly ere she died; and that he never forgot her, and honoured her all the days of his life, for that she freely gave her life, only that he might live.

FROM THE VOLSUNGASAGA

Part three

1

Holy Island

June 1065

n principio.

The boy sat on a grassy outcrop surmounting the cliffs that bordered this edge of the holy island, watching, far below, the sea's timeless work of erosion, as each green wave creamed into white foam against wet, black rock, wearing away its intractable surface. The screeching gulls that nested in the rocks, and the sleek black cormorants that wheeled over the waves, were his only companions. His eyes closed against the hard blue sky, dark thundery clouds building up from the west, he could hear only that restless rhythmic motion of advance and retreat, assault and withdrawal; the surging clash and splatter of a broken wave, and the hoarse sigh of the retiring tide as it withdrew, sucking and breathing, over the rattling shingle.

The boy assumed that it was because he had never left the island that the sound, smell and motion of the sea provoked in his heart such emotions of nostalgia and desire. He knew that he had come across that ocean, from the east, as a tiny baby; but the sea, although the means of his advent, represented also the barrier between himself and his past. He had reached the island out of that great salt source of fertility, strange sterile creator, as inexplicably as a new human soul finds itself delivered from the salt sea of its mother's womb. Though it lives, comfortably enough, in the new world of its deliverance, the soul is never free from an unappeasable hunger for some other world it has lost, or from a powerful sense of birth as a shipwreck, a profound and irreparable disaster. Why did he feel that, happy as he was, his true home was somewhere else, somewhere far away across that barrier of wave-surging, tide-swollen water?

The only language available to him was that of his religious education, which depicted every individual soul as equally abandoned, cut off by the original sin from the God who was both father and mother, maker and deliverer, rescue and hope. Perhaps that was why, as he sat on the bare edge of his known world, he was, on occasion, overwhelmed by that inconsolable longing to be re-united with the author of his being, to return to the father, to go home.

And so he wandered back to the huddle of communal buildings he had come to know as his home, and entered the monastery church, feeling as soon as he stepped into the hushed and darkened interior, lit only by the multicoloured light that filtered or streamed through the stained-glass windows, elaborately wrought by Roman craftsmen, a familiar sense of consolation. He breathed the soft, moist air, heavily perfumed with incense, and knelt before the one bright object in the otherwise pervasive gloom, a gilded crucifix, with five bright jewels, representing the five wounds of Christ, set into its cross-beam. There, in both formal prayers and personal meditations, he could fill his mind with the image of God as a caring father, from whose love nothing, neither in life nor in death, could ever separate him; and of that only begotten Son whom, because He so loved the world, the loving Father freely gave. His wound of violent separation was soothed by an image of the sustaining hands (in which one could place an absolute trust, and through which it was impossible to fall) of the living God. There he could sense a keen companionship from contemplation of the Son's own exile and dispossession, as he cried out on the cross to the Father who had forsaken him.

There also within the fertile darkness, in the adjoining space of her own chapel, was the image of the mother, the blue-cloaked Holy Virgin whose round womb recalled the annunciation of her pregnancy, and testified to that dark creative power, the Holy Ghost, whose inexplicable act of procreation brought love and redemption into the world.

Temporarily at home among the personalities of this divine family, he would study the vivid and stirring iconography of the great stained-glass windows that dominated the chancel: the figure of Christ in majesty, presiding over the whole narrative of creation and fall, redemption and judgement, past, present and future. Though His hands were stretched out towards the spectator, wounded palms held outwards in a gesture of helpless abandonment to love, yet from His left hand sprang a vision of Eden, the Tree of Life set in a bright green paradise, the naked figures of Adam and Eve tending its branches. Then below, a poignant image of those hapless sinners cast out from the garden, their nakedness shamefully clothed, Adam's face hidden in his hands, Eve's raised in open, inconsolable grief to the unforgiving heavens, a blinding brightness of angelic swords guarding the now inaccessible east. There followed, in descending sequence, the Old Testament narratives of the Flood, and the Tower of Babel, the heroic legends of David and Samson; until, from the lowest pane, sprang the root of the cross itself, rising in agony and splendour to dominate the window's centre. The left-hand panels traced upwards the life of Jesus, through scenes of miracle and teaching, betrayal and sacrifice, concluding with the Ascension; and a final panel showed the deliverance, at the Last Judgement, of all human souls into His pitying, yet stern, judicial hand.

What a piece of work! Express and admirable, crafted by human hands, the window revealed the beauty of the world: the actions of angels, the apprehension of gods. Yet within its frame man appeared as little more than a quintessence of dust. One panel the boy found particularly moving was that depicting the first murder, the slaughter of Abel by his brother Cain. Cain stood alone, arraigned before God's judgement, in his hand a bloodstained stone. The murdered corpse of his innocent brother was nowhere to be seen. The offence was rank, it smelt to heaven: for slaughtered Abel's blood cried out to God from beneath the ground, pleading for justice. Where could a man hide the shadow of his blood-guiltiness, the crime of a brother's murder? Could those mute sealed cavities, the graves of the dead, open again to expel their occupants? Could those thirsty fissures gape to release a thin lamenting ghost? Could those caverns echo and amplify a silent cry for revenge, bestow on wronged silence a living voice?

2
Neaʀ Helsingoʀ

June 1065

ortinbras had indicated clearly enough, immediately after Hamlet's funeral, that Horatio would be detained on diplomatic business for some considerable time. Horatio was, however, able to measure his own underestimation of the suspicion with which Fortinbras regarded him, by the length of time the king kept him engaged in matters of foreign policy, sending him ever further abroad on more intractable political problems. What with missions to England to resolve disputes over Danegeld; to the court of the Emperor in an attempt to settle feuds between families in Norway and Germany; and as far away as Rome to solicit the Holy Father's blessing on Fortinbras's marriage to the young Swedish princess, it was ten years before he found himself touching, with the soft bump of a boat's prow, his home shores, and breathing again his cold native air. Glancing up at the cliffs above the harbour, he saw again the black edifice of the royal tomb from which the body of his loved lord had all those years ago been secretly conveyed and dispatched on its last long voyage.

A brief interview with Fortinbras, in the course of which the king bestowed profuse thanks, and offered ample reward for the services so loyally delivered, was enough to advise Horatio that he was no longer regarded as a significant threat.

He had attended the king in his council chamber, where he sat, surrounded by scribes and advisors, at a table covered in state papers. Fortinbras seemed so preoccupied with business matters that Horatio considered withdrawing to return later. When the king eventually looked up, he seemed hardly to recognise his envoy. But when Horatio knelt in homage and introduced himself, Fortinbras rose from the table and greeted him with what seemed like genuine courtesy.

The king had offered Horatio rewards of wealth, but he had refused them, as he always did, having no use for land or treasure. Indeed he was anxious to avoid the danger and responsibility riches would entail. In this particular instance, he had no wish to reawaken, by assuming the properties of wealth and power, Fortinbras's slumbering suspicions. The precaution might well have been unnecessary, for Fortinbras had clearly ruled out Horatio as a serious threat to his now well-established kingdom. If anything, he seemed to have developed an admiration for the man who had transferred his loyalty so willingly, yet had given as true and honest service to his new master as he had to the old. Though there might well be future activities upon which he would wish Horatio to be engaged, for the present, the king intimated, he could consider himself again a private individual, at liberty to avail himself of the privileges of the court, or of the literary resources of Denmark's churches and monasteries. Horatio had thanked him with a respectfully deep but somewhat stiff bow, betokening both the weariness of travel and a careful effort of concealment, lest the true delights of liberty should display themselves in some relaxation of muscle or alacrity of limb.

Now the red sun was flooding the tops of the eastern pines as Horatio reined his horse at the top of a rocky trail. Below in the valley bottom the stream etched its thin, deep line, its waters flowing green and swift, swollen by the spring rains. Further down the valley, he knew, where it narrowed and concentrated to force itself through a tight rocky cleft, before precipitating into a short waterfall, was the spot where poor Ofelia had sought her release in muddy death. Beyond the fall the stream broadened into a wide-skirted pool where reeds fringed the dark water, and where the rising of carp to spring flies traced on the surface an endless series of rippling eddies. At the edge of the weir-pool stood the monastery church whose brothers had, according to the Queen's account, intercepted and withdrawn her cold, floating body. Allowing his horse to pick a careful path between the white stones of the trail, Horatio followed the stream's course, mentally preparing the questions he hoped would elicit the answers he sought.

As he entered the glade where the monastery had stood, he perceived immediately that it was there no more. Nothing but tumbled stones, grey ash. White flakes that stirred and lifted on the gentle spring breeze. The scorched ruins still marked out in a cruciform shape the vanished bulk of the old church. Fire had with ravenous appetite consumed timber and glass, reduced to ruin metal and stone. Horatio could see, in his mind's eye, the stained-glass windows pop and burst, runnels of lead trickling down the scorched walls. He saw a bright gold crucifix, enveloped in flames, sag and liquefy in the conflagration's hot breath.

Then, afterwards, the building's stones, mortar eroded and timber reduced to ash, would collapse and return to anonymous rubble. Vegetation, patiently working its way through the remnants of human cultivation, already sprang liberally among the stones. Any remnants of value, bits of melted gold and bright imperishable gems, had long since been plundered by searching hands. Very soon the traces of what had stood there would disappear beneath clambering undergrowth and trailing weeds.

What had happened? Accident? Natural disaster? Had the community vanished before the building, perhaps decimated by disease, or riven by schism? Or did the past hoard among its treasury of secrets some more deliberate and focused cause than these random and innocent explanations? No one could deny that here fate had exerted some of its irresistible influence. But fate used many methods of securing its destined ends, among them the deliberate actions of men. Could Horatio discern, somewhere behind this calamity, a mailed fist raised in judgement or revenge? In purge or persecution?

The breeze lifted and dispersed white ashes that resembled Horatio's thoughts, beginning to evaporate into indistinctness. What now? Where now, but to follow the wind to the west?

3
Holy Island

June 1065

Cold northern light pierced the rough stone embrasure and struck hard across a solid wooden chessboard, the only object resting on the surface of a crudely hewn plank table. The boy sat leaning forward, chin in hands: his fair hair cut in a straight fringe over wide, cold blue eyes; his attention concentrated on the big chess figures that were drawn up in neat formation at either end of the board.

Though he had thoroughly learned the rules of chess, their elaborate conventions and arbitrary logic held no interest for him. Why should this piece have power to move in this direction, but not that? Or move so many squares, and no more? The military discipline of the game bored him. Like mathematics, chess was too chaste and abstract for his taste.

His imagination was absorbed rather by the carved chess figures themselves, roughly sculpted in pure ivory,

cut from the tusks of a huge walrus speared off the Greenland coast. Each figure squatted heavily, body and head
leaning forward over the knees, hands clasped in various
attitudes, faces alive with grotesque expression. In particular the boy was fascinated by the figures of king and
queen: the king with short sword across his knees,
gripped at hilt and point, hollow-eyed and sad; the queen
with a hand clasped beside a face contorted with an
expression of violent fear.

The mystery of the pieces seemed to lie folded within
their solid mass, illegibly inscribed in an unfamiliar language, yet emanating a sense of obscure power. What terrible experience had made the king so drawn with
sadness, his eyes empty with pain, insensible even to the
edge of the blade his fingers grappled? And the queen:
what image of horror disfigured her face, gripped her
locked arms in such taut extremity?

The space between the figures was as interesting to the
boy as the pieces themselves; but not as mere borders
demarcating territories, the chequer-work of diplomacy.
The lines and squares of the board were the spaces of an
invisible power that kept the pieces apart and delineated
their relations to one another. It was the arbitrary stagger-
ing of one square that kept a king safe, the accidental
opening of a direct passage that threw him into immediate danger. The boy removed the kings', queens' and
bishops' pawns to the edge of the board, disclosing a
dangerous itinerary of squares between the rival monarchies. Queen faced queen and king king: red challenged
white. King and queen stared at one another across

emptiness: sadness confronted fear.

The boy felt the white queen pulling towards the red king, drawn to him by a silent magnetism. The king could move only one square towards her, passing in front of his own queen: but she was tugged towards him by a charismatic force that provoked passions of destructiveness and desire. She wanted him; but she wanted him destroyed. The boy slowly slid the white queen towards the red king. Her partner sat hunched in white immobility, paralysed by her independent movement. Now she neared the king, stopping one square short to exert her power in safety. The red queen sat immovable behind her king, mouth wrenched open sideways in a silent scream. The red king felt secure in the protection afforded by his consort: he knew his assailant, the blanched snow-queen, could not destroy him without annihilating herself, as the snow melts before the red sun.

The intervening square emanated a dark field of force, generated by the silent struggle, but in turn confining the participants in a network of their own power. Regardless of rules, the boy charged the force of the square still further by moving the white king to a square adjacent to that occupied by his queen. The kings were equally repelled and attracted by the resistance they provoked. What was the power of that empty space that was capable of keeping them apart, locked in a potent tension, but frozen into inactivity? Why could the two kings not occupy adjacent squares? Why could they not rule together in friendship and love, like brothers?

The lines of force operating across the square filled it

with a dark strength, invisible but potent, like a black star, or like the jaws of that great wolf, son of Fenrir, who would in the final days swallow the sun. Exhausted by power, war-weary, the two kings looked sadly on one another. As their reciprocal sorrow welled out into the square, the horror on the faces of their queens became more intelligible. Is that all there is to being a king – endless exertion of empty power, then betrayal, defeat, supersession? How weary, stale, flat and unprofitable seem the uses of this world! Fie on't! Fie! It is an unweeded garden that grows to seed; things rank and gross in nature do possess it merely. The square seemed to glow with a dark fire, hum with a soft vibration, like the northern lights.

The boy could feel the white king's spirit slowly ebbing in weariness, could feel the lapsing of his force. His red brother watched and waited, tasting victory. Resigned to defeat, the white king's sorrowful countenance drooped. Where was his queen, his chaste and innocent white snowbride? Look to her, Hamlet ...

4
Helsingor

June 1065

Horatio tethered his horse to a chipped and battered marble headstone at the edge of the royal cemetery.

Pausing only to cross himself before the imperial monu-
ment, he picked his way through the jumbled litter of
gravestones that crammed an open space circumscribed
by the more substantial tombs of landed families, and of
military and ecclesiastical leaders. Segregated, as they had
been in life, by wealth and privilege, into rich and poor,
beneath the ground Denmark's dead seemed all equal citi-
zens of the same dark kingdom, a homogenised mass of
ruined mortality, where the toe of the peasant rubbed
uncomfortably against the heel of the courtier. Clambering over the rear wall of the grave yard, Horatio followed a
path leading into a thick covert, within which was concealed, in an open clearing, a tumble down stone hovel. By
the door, taking the early sun, sat an old man, chin on
hands, gnarled knuckles cupped around a carved stick. His
face was the texture of old leather and his toothless jaws
folded neatly the one over the other. But his bright black
eyes retained all the cunning that had evidently charac-
terised an intelligent younger self.

A young woman emerged from the cottage, a daughter
taking care of her infirm and elderly father.

'Why, sir, did you seek my father? There he is, indeed,
though little speech you will hear from him. Dumb he's
been, quite wordless, now, for nigh on fifteen year – since
our young Prince Hamlet died, God rest his soul. He hears
well enough, and knows what and where, though he be all
of sixty year of age. There he sits, all the livelong day. God
knows but what he do deserve some peace in his old age.
He was sexton here for thirty years, man and boy, and
buried many a lord and lady, nay kings and queens too.

He came to it that day that Old King Amled overcame Fortenbrasse ...'

Horatio sat down beside the old man, in a chair provided for him by the garrulous daughter. The old man returned his stare, though there was no sign in the brilliant black eyes of any recognition or understanding.

'Do you remember me, my friend?' Horatio asked.

An expression crinkled the deep-set eyes, perhaps only of caution and cunning, perhaps of recollection.

'You did a service for me, once, you remember. Though not, in truth, for me, but out of love and respect for the young Prince Hamlet, whom you served, and for his great father before him. And now', Horatio leaned closer to the old man, his mouth almost touching the listening ear, 'there is another service you can do, for the memory of your Prince, and for the glory of his father's name'.

He continued for some time to whisper into the old man's ear.

'Noble King Edwin' said one of his courtiers: 'let us compare this present life of man on earth to that great universe of time and space of which we have no knowledge.

'Imagine yourself, on a cold winter's evening, sitting in your banqueting hall, brightly lit by torches and warmed by fires, surrounded by your thegns and counsellors. Outside, storms of winter rain and snow are raging.

'Then, through one of the doors, in flies a sparrow, flitting in rapid, zigzag flight through the hall. As long as he remains in the hall, he shares your world of safety and protection, light and warmth; he is safe from the blasts of winter and the dread of darkness. But soon these few seconds of comfort are over: he flies out through the other door and vanishes from our sight, back into that wintry world from whence he came.

'Even so is the life of man. For a brief space he appears here on earth, and enjoys its comforts and its benefits. Then he is gone, and earth knows him no more. Like the sparrow, he came, none knows how, from that great unfathomable space of cold and darkness; and like the sparrow, he returns to it again, to God knows where.

'Our own world, we know; but of what comes before and after, we know nothing.'

FROM BEDE, ECCLESIASTICAL
HISTORY OF THE ENGLISH PEOPLE

At midnight, visible only as a tangle of shadows beneath a sky half-lit by an untidy drift of stars and the pale phosphorescence of a waning moon, the cemetery was a very different place. What seemed, at bright noonday, a peaceful silence, was here transformed into a roused and bristling darkness.

Under the broad daylight sky the graveyard was an open and public space, marked out within the delineated territories of human civilisation as a quiet resting place for the dead. Here, among this litter of fractured stones, death appeared as the cold, empty space in which all human hope and achievement ultimately come to dust and ashes. 'Man that is born of woman hath but a short time to live, and is full of misery'. From this quiet ground every soul, in those terrible last days, would emerge from the tomb, blinking in the blinding light of a new heaven, to deliver a final account of its life on earth. Here was the place where human power would be surrendered to the terrifying might of the Lord in judgement.

But in the darkness the cemetery appeared rather as a gateway opening onto another domain, a forgotten kingdom where neither God nor man seemed to reign as sovereign lord of all the world. There in that moving blackness dwelt the creatures of ancestral fear, the ogres and elves, monsters and giants, Cain's evil kin who bore God's wrath. From the fenland haunts of their dark homeland they jealously watched the bright lights of the hall and enviously heard the clear voice of the harper, singing the song of

God's Creation. Seeing, for a moment, with their tor-
mented eyes, the tiny and isolated space of human habita-
tion, winking like a wind-blown candle in the great
darkness, Horatio was momentarily chilled by a deep and
atavistic timidity. He remembered once reading of human
life, with its bright brief span, as like a sparrow flitting
from outer darkness into the brilliant torch-lit cheerful-
ness of the mead hall, only to re-enter by the opposite
window the night that was its true eternal home. Yet as
his dead master had once observed, there may be a providence in the fall even of a sparrow.

Though the healthy scepticism and intellectual arro-
gance of youth, that had formerly inoculated Horatio
against other-wordly fears, had long since evaporated
from his mind, even here he felt no particular terror. He
had no apprehension that the sheeted dead would suddenly rise before him, squeaking and gibbering, merely to
freeze his blood and stop his heart with fear. For he had
passed, in one unforgettable night, from one who would
smile with wry amusement at ghost stories and tales of
the dark, to one who knew that the dead, though real and
capable of apparition, have no leisure for trivial hauntings
or the scaring of children. A dead soul will be awakened
from its long sleep only by the most urgent summons, and
would revisit the earth only on the most imperative of
quests.

Ahead of him, the old man carefully picked his way
between the jumble of gravestones and collapsed sar-
cophagi, lighting his path by the fitful flame of a shaded
lantern. A small wind stirred the trees, scattering faint

starlight across broken tombs. Horatio followed obediently, trusting by some instinct that his guide's sense and
memory were still as strong and intact as his bright eyes
were sharply intelligent, and not as dilapidated as the
arthritic joints and stooping body.

The old man stopped, and held out his lantern for Horatio to see. In a terrace of facaded tombs, the scarred
stucco of an originally impressive mausoleum now presented a history of desuetude and neglect, its blistered
and peeling exterior eloquent of dynastic extinction and
encroaching oblivion. This, Horatio guessed, was the tomb
of the Polonius family. This was where the corpse of the
old counsellor lay nursing in his tight shroud the secret of
his death-wound; and where beside him lay his young son,
Laertes, body as shrivelled by venom as his soul had been
warped by hatred. Here, Horatio assumed, the remains of
poor Ofelia would have been interred after her funeral
rites had broken up in undignified brawling.

But the old man did not, as Horatio expected, bend to
open the iron gate of the Polonius tomb but hobbled
around behind it, into a narrow strip of waste ground
that had obviously been employed, as occupancy of the
graveyard steadily increased, to hold the remains of the
less privileged departed. Here rotten wooden crosses, or
unshaped stones crudely etched with runic inscriptions,
marked the graves of the poor, of slaves, of prisoners
unworthy of ransom, all buried in the old fashion with
feet and hands tied together.

A big oblong slab of slate with no markings indicated
to Horatio that here, in a deep anonymous pit, had been

unceremoniously cast the bodies of plague victims. To his surprise, it was by this slab that the sexton paused, bent down and, with remarkable reserves of strength, slid the stone sideways to reveal a flight of roughly hewn steps that adjoined the rear wall of the Polonius tomb. Then he disappeared downwards into the darkness, beckoning Horatio to follow.

In the uncertain light of the lantern, Horatio was aware on his left of the stone foundations of the tomb, walling in the crypt; on his right, the crumbling interior of the plague pit, with here and there a brown, shrivelled bone of foot or finger protruding from the congealed soil. The old man obviously had no more fear of lingering infection than had the plump rats who retreated, squeaking, before their descent. It was beyond doubt, on the other hand, that the fearful respect with which the human community regarded the hapless victims of the pestilence, that made this, if indeed it was so, a supremely reliable place of concealment.

But if this was Ofelia's final resting place, what had brought her here? Did the priest who conducted her truncated obsequies propitiate his own scruples by burying her, notwithstanding the power of royal command, in unconsecrated ground? Or had the corpse been removed from its proper interment in the family vault to evade some previous attempt to locate it? Was Horatio following in the footsteps of a predecessor who had attempted some parallel pursuit?

At the foot of the stairs a low, bricked-up archway indicated a rear entrance to the tomb. But again, this was not the old man's destination. Instead he squatted down in a hollow scooped out beneath the plague pit, and, setting down his lantern, began to scrape with his hands at the loose earth, uncovering a small stone panel that proved to be the end of a deeply interred sarcophagus. Working the square end loose, he removed it and set it aside. Then reaching with the full length of his arms into the cavity, he slid towards himself a bier on which lay a corpse, covered in rich grave-cloths, now earth-stained and yellow with age.

Gently, almost with tenderness, he loosened the coverings around the corpse's face, then squatted back on his heels. Horatio bent down to inspect the remains, and with a shock of mingled pity and horror beheld the face of Ofelia, clearly identifiable, but no longer the face of the young woman he now vividly remembered. The skin had tightened around the jaw and cheekbones, the hair had rotted to untidy wisps around the brown bald scalp, the lips had shrivelled and the eye sockets wrinkled and puckered, so that the face he saw was the face of Ofelia as the old woman she had never survived to become. Strange that the processes of decay, in life and in death, should produce such similar results!

The old man was observing Horatio critically, as if appraising his strength of character. Then he crooked a finger to draw him down to the mouth the grave. Taking Horatio's right hand in strong, blunt fingers, he guided it down among the folds of the shroud to touch the surface of the corpse's neck and chest. Struggling to overcome his revulsion, Horatio allowed his hand to be taken and drawn down into that inconceivable darkness. His gorge rose as his fingers touched the dry skin of an empty, wrinkled breast. Then disgust gave way to a sudden access of compassion, shot through with exhilaration of discovery, as he felt beneath the corpse's ribs the out-turned lips of a massive scar. Fingering its length towards the groin, he felt the transverse cicatrice that bisected the torso from hip to hip.

'Conception is a blessing'. But not as *this* daughter had conceived.

5
Holy Island

December 1065

*I*n *principio*. The faint scratch of a nib on vellum. The creak of a chair and the rustle of a habit across a cramped, out-stretched arm. A sigh of weariness. A muttered prayer: *Ave Maria, Gratia Plena, Dominus Tecum*. Silence, and the insect-like scratching resumed. An odour of incense stole across the harsh tang of leather and the pungent scent of ink.

The boy was in the *scriptorium* with its adjoining library, examining some of the newly completed pages which the monks, with their tireless dedication, were copying or re-fashioning. There on a lectern lay an illuminated page of St John's gospel, its colour still drying, its bold brightness and elaborate decoration arresting the eye. This was not scripture as narrative or teaching but scripture as object and event. The whole page contained only a handful of words. But what words!

In principio erat verbum et verbum erat apud deum et deus erat verbum*

The three initial letters, I, n, p, were knitted into a massive, statuesque form that dominated the page, sealed at its ends by great flourishes like architectural pedestals, or the flowering tips of a king's sceptre. Everywhere within the strict geometric lines of the design were fluid and mobile signs of vitality, creeping undulating plants, two-headed beasts knotted together in vibrant symbiosis, strange, exotic birds, their bodies intertwined in an ecstasy of love. Even the simplest decorative motif displayed that irrepressible tendency towards organic unity, shapes interleaved and lines interlaced, as if all creation were seeking to resolve and re-combine into some lost pristine solidarity.

The English monk who had illuminated the manuscript had introduced an interlinear vernacular translation of the Vulgate text, as if the Latin scripture was already more a remote poetry than a modern gospel:

In prima wor word and word wor mid god fader and word wor god

But the paraphrase seemed a banal attenuation of that brilliant red, green and yellow incarnation of the word in image and design, which seemed to declare, in immediate sensuous apprehension, the presence of God in the world,

---

* 'In the beginning was the Word, and the Word was with God, and the Word was God' (John, 1.1)

and the undeniable reality of Creation. 'Word wor god': the Word at work in the world.

Beside the gospel page lay another leaf of manuscript, part of a collection of poems, chronicles and homilies, in English and Latin, which were undergoing collation into a single multifarious codex. One poem arrested his attention, one of the old English elegies that sang so poignantly of exile and wandering; of a bitter present, a bright lost past, and a longed-for eternal future.

Oft him anhaga. are gebidath. metudes miltse ...[*]

The boy lingered over the manuscript, sounding each alliterative line in a silent rapture: hearing, in the modulated cadences, the sound and motion of the sea itself, the wanderer's only home. This was a poetry that struck deep to his very soul. For though in the confident faith of the illuminated gospel he could grasp creation's exuberant mastery: for him there was no '*in principio*', since of his own origins and antecedents he remained ignorant. So here, in the sadness of the old song, he discovered one of his soul's authentic voices.

[*]   'How often a loner longs for the Lord, looks for his love...'

6
The Alps

June 1065

Horato's first glimpse of the mountain monastery was from deep within the fertile cleft of a valley separating two high peaks. There it was, high in the air, balanced precariously on the edge of a chalk escarpment: pale sandstone walls, a bright red-tiled roof, and a squat tower that seemed unwilling, as if in humility, to soar to any greater height.

All the way from the valley bed where they were pitching camp, unharnessing the pack mules and breaking out provisions, clusters of forestation swarmed upwards, piled like cloud on cloud, overlapping in irrepressible growth, stopping short only at the very summit where a stony, eroded outcrop afforded no soil for roots to gain a purchase. Hence the old church occupied a tonsured eminence of rock and seemed to hover there in an unreality of thin bright air. Nearer to God were its inhabitants at that elevation, reflected Horatio: and equally further away from men. It seemed no accident that the mountain solitude deemed necessary for daily transactions with the divine, also shielded the community from exposure to the curious eyes of any but the hardiest of climbers, the most persistent of guests.

Seeing their destination etched so distinctly against

the evening sky, Horatio in his eagerness to arrive was surprised that they did not press on to the summit and avail
themselves of shelter against the bitter-cold mountain
night. His guides explained that this was an illusion of the
mountain air, that the monastery in truth remained distant a whole day's march, and that the visitor's unaccustomed eyes were cancelling the intervening space to bring
the desired object closer than it really was.

Night came up the pass like a rising flood, and when it
reached the summit the monastery resembled a vessel
tossed on shadowy seas. Red sunset drained from mountain peaks, leaving them white and distant in the gathering gloom. Horatio sat by the campfire and waited for his
companions to drop into silent drowsiness. He too was
weary but a necessary vigilance propped open his aching
eyes. Just before his departure from Geneva, as he waited
at the inn door for the transport beast to be brought
round from the stables, a messenger had slipped out of
the shadows and thrust a packet in his hand. Horatio had
just glimpsed, in the torchlight shed from the open door,
the corner of a fair beard and moustache, almost concealed beneath a heavy black cowl, before the man disappeared as quickly into the darkness. He had had no
privacy on the long journey through the mountain passes
in which to consult the contents and now took the opportunity of unsealing the whaleskin packet and extracting a
letter which he bent down to read by the dull red glow of
dying wood embers.

The letter was written in runic characters, to decipher
which Horatio had to ransack his ancestral memories. No

little ingenuity was also required to unlock the secure cryptic code within which the missive's meaning was tightly enfolded. After interpreting only the first few characters, however, he knew that this was news he had been waiting for.

From a Faithful servant of Christ to the Freeman Horatio

To my dear friend Horatio, the blessings of God's grace, and greetings from your people who have found peace in this wild and beautiful land. It is my fervent hope that you may by the time this reaches you have found that which we both have lost, and hunger to recover.

Your letters have reached me safely, here in my ice-home, and have kindled in an old man's heart a hope that will burn until death extinguishes its fire. Many of your friends and mine, brothers and sisters in Christ, who occupy with me this island solitude, share my expectations, and long once again to look upon him whom, having not seen, they yet love, and rejoice with joy unspeakable at the hope of voyaging with him to the kingdom.

Until we meet again, and begin our voyage home, I rest your faithful servant.

The letter was signed with the shape of a cross, the foot of its shaft bisected by the image of a hammer. Horatio smiled at the ingenuity with which Thorsten – his name encrypted in the symbol of Thor's hammer – had employed to secure his meaning. Had the letter fallen into enemy hands, it would have appeared to be a straightforward communication to Horatio from a group of

Christians who had retreated to the contemplative life on some barren northern island. Even the hammer would have put the reader in mind of the tools of the crucifixion, rather than the hammer of the Norse gods. But the message told Horatio that Thorsten was, as he had suspected, settled in Iceland (his 'ice-home') with an army and was ready at any moment to embark on a quest to recover his homeland for a new king.

Nor would it have represented an unusual circumstance for Horatio to receive such a message. Even since his return to Denmark he had, as everyone knew, taken a great interest in matters of religion and spent most of his time visiting convents and monasteries in Scandinavia and the adjoining territories. Though his initial motivation seemed a scholarly one, his purpose to gain access to the treasures of monastic libraries, he soon developed a reputation for piety and religious dedication. When asked by old friends of the Danish court if he intended to take the vows himself, Horatio would demur with a downcast modesty that confirmed rather than denied his questioner's suspicions.

Horatio had carefully developed this persona as a cover for his search. Knowing that Queen Gertrude had been a prominent patroness of the monastic orders in Denmark, he had guessed that Ofelia's child, it if had lived, would most likely have been spirited away into monastic keeping. Hence his search began intensively with monasteries in Denmark, then eventually broadened to include the wider world of Europe. He would arrive at a monastery, avail himself of the brothers' hospitality, spend time in the library and *scriptorium*, join the monks at their regular devotions. Then gradually, subtly, his inquiries would open. But nowhere did he find anything of specific application, though everywhere he encountered rumours of a child, born to Prince Hamlet and the Lady Ofelia, a son who had either perished or been lost into the anonymity of folklore. Horatio judged that those most willing to disclose such speculations were those with no genuine knowledge or detailed information. So he would leave after a few days, none the wiser, more convinced of the hopelessness of his quest.

But he never entirely lost hope, and gradually as his journey took him westwards, there grew on him an imperceptible sensation of arrival, of drawing near his destination. Perhaps it was nothing more than the fact that the rumours concerning the lost Prince of Denmark seemed to diminish, as if people knew more than they were prepared to say. Though what else could he expect, as he travelled further from his own land, than a reduction of interest in its history and legend? Perhaps hope grew stronger, flourishing in a vacuum of absence, the more strongly life seemed to refute it.

Now he could not control a growing excitement, buoyed up by Thorsten's letter, but somehow stimulated by the first glimpse of that strange anchorite's eyrie, the eyes of its narrow windows glancing down into the deep valleys below, the finger of its tower aiming at heaven; like an image of Christ, looking down in pity, pointing upwards in hope and love. So although the last to retire to rest, Horatio was the first to rise at dawn, eager to depart.

How many more surges of hope and shocks of disappointment could his heart take, before its youthful elasticity began to harden into despair? Perhaps here, in this mountain fastness, so close to heaven: perhaps there, on that consecrated peak, he who had lost so much would find his reward.

It was almost dark again by the time they neared the summit. The climb had been hard and hot, and often they had paused to drink from achingly cold streams of melted ice and snow. Now as the heat of the glowing day changed to the searching cold of the rarefied night air, so the wooded slopes gave way to desolation. No trees could find root, and all that grew here was a scrubby brown moss frozen into the interstices of rock. As the first mule of the train slipped up the craggy causeway to the gates of the monastery, they opened, throwing a solid beam of light across the stony slope where ice crystals sparkled and gleamed. Silent monks emerged to take their beasts by the bridles and to help the guides unload.

Horatio was invited in and led by a speechless cowled figure up a great stone staircase, through chilly corridors to a chamber where he was able to wash and change. The monk waited outside for him and when he was ready beckoned him to follow. Their destination was a chamber door at the end of a corridor. The monk tapped respectfully at the door and bowed to indicate that Horatio should enter.

In a large chamber, heated by a big log fire, sat a monk who was obviously, by his air of quiet authority, the Abbott of the place. He was writing, thick glass spectacles perched on the end of his nose. He gestured to Horatio to take a seat by the fire and with no sign of urgency finished his writing. Then he rose from the table, poured wine from a beaten copper jug into a pewter goblet, and handed it to Horatio, who drank its contents with gratitude. Finally the Abbott took a chair opposite Horatio, and looked at him for the first time.

Horatio found himself opposite a man who would hardly have been taken for a monk, had it not been for the black habit of his order. His face was smooth and highly coloured, the jawline large but still firm, the blue eyes subtle with intelligence and humour. On his breast he wore a big pectoral cross. Horatio had encountered such men before, but always in different circumstances. He resembled a bishop of some substantial diocese in one of the countries, Italy or Germany, where the church had wealth and power. He was a man who seemed to live well, not a creature of abstinence. He exuded a confident power, rather then the prickly humility Horatio would have expected in an Abbott ruling over so remote and inaccessible a community.

The monk's address to Horatio was startlingly simple and unceremonious:

'You are seeking something, my friend: but to save you time, I will tell you that you will not find it here'.

The monk smiled at his discomfiture.

'There is hardly any need to beat about the bush. We

are men of the world, you and I, and we know how the world goes. Do not imagine, that we are in our remoteness in any way out of touch.

'The church lives in movement and communication. We travel to carry the gospel to those not yet blessed by God's grace. We keep in constant contact with our brethren in other lands. We bear comfort to them when they are in distress; and we receive with delight the news of their successes.

'You can hardly expect us not to carry with us on our travels that commodity that nowadays all men seek: intelligence, information. The church lives at peace with all its neighbours. We did not burn Rome: we went meekly into the arena at the behest of he who did. We are not so stupid as to interfere overtly in affairs of state. But we are also clever enough to know that knowledge is power.

'So yes, I know all about you, Horatio, and about your quest. Be not afraid: I will betray you to no one. But neither, I fear, can I assist you'.

He rose and went back to the table to help himself and Horatio to wine. He resumed his speech while walking about the room, as if uncomfortable with the awkwardness of his words.

'Today Denmark is at peace. Men live without fearing for their lives. The church is not persecuted. We expect little from any earthly king except to be let alone to do God's work. Why should it matter to us if one king or another rules?'

He paused in his pacing and stood before Horatio.

'I want you to go from here, not just with a brief disappointment, and a will to renew your search. I want you to believe that your search is over. You are a good man, and a friend of the church. Accept God's will. It is a new parable: that which is lost will never be found. Let old quarrels lie where they belong, in the pages of history. Give up, my friend. Resign yourself to failure. Go home'.

There was something in Horatio's voice as he quietly and ironically repeated the words 'Go home!' that arrested the Abbott's attention. He looked at the traveller and the despair on his face smote the monk to the heart.

'I have no home', said Horatio, softly and without self-pity, as if merely stating a fact. 'My home is hope; my life has become my quest. Take hope from me, and you render me homeless; rob me of my quest and you may as well take away my life'.

He rose as if to take his leave, moving blindly across the room towards the door. As he reached it, his hand on the latch, he heard the Abbott speak, sharply and in a changed tone: 'Stop'. There was a long pause while he walked over to the window and stared out at a cloud-stained darkness littered with a smattering of stars.

'I cannot see a soul in despair, and not offer what help I can. Come with me'.

Seizing a candlestick, he preceded Horatio from the chamber. Following him along the draughty corridors, Horatio could hear from below the melancholy chanting of vespers in the abbey church. Candlelight flickered on the old walls. The monk reached a door, and turned to address Horatio.

'This one thing I will do for you, out of pity for your

sorrow and respect for your cause. Here in this room is the one man who can, if any can, reveal the answer to your riddle.

'But I warn you: no one has yet found the information you seek. Perhaps it will never be found. What you find in this room may persuade you more effectively than my words to abandon your quest'.

He pushed the door open, and Horatio followed him in. The chamber was a small cell, with bare whitewashed walls and a skylight set high in the vaulted roof, through which cascaded a slim beam of moonlight. The only furniture in the room was a bed, and on it Horatio could see in the candlelight the face of an old man, asleep or dead. On the wall opposite the bed was a black wooden crucifix.

'Brother Tostig was the only survivor of the massacre that purged the monastery of Helsingor. When the Norwegian troops surrounded the church, he hid in a cellar. Though the monastery was sacked and burnt to the ground, the Lord saw fit to spare him. He sustained terrible injuries, but he lived, and managed in the darkness to escape and make his way to friends who nursed him back to what little health he has. Eventually he was brought here. His throat and lungs were burned as he lay in the charring ruins, so he has no power of speech. But those who brought him here swore that he told his rescuers, by signs or writing, that with him in that dreadful conflagration was a child, an infant he protected with his own body. He took the baby, it is said, to other loyal brethren, and bade them transport it to safety. Since he has been here, he has uttered no word, nor made any sign that could be understood. No one knows the whereabouts of the lost child.

'I will permit you to speak with him for five minutes. After that, I will bid you goodnight, for you will be gone in the morning. God go with you'.

Abruptly he left the room, leaving Horatio with the silent moonlit figure on the bed.

Horatio knelt on the cold flags beside the bed and scrutinised the old man's face. The scar of a huge burn seared his right cheek, and his throat and chest were similarly disfigured. Staring at the purple scars beneath the white hair of his chest, Horatio became aware that the man was awake and staring at him with black eyes that glinted in the moonlight. Without saying a word, Horatio drew from inside his doublet a gold locket on a long chain. The monk's eyes fixed on it, and his throat opened to emit a hoarse groan. Horatio flipped open the locket and held up before the searching eyes the portrait of King Amled.

Tears filled the old man's eyes and ran down into the white stubble of his ruined jaw. He clutched at Horatio's arm, and leaned up to reach his ear. His breath foetid against Horatio's cheek, he breathed with immense effort a single word. Then his hand slackened, his eyes closed and he fell back onto the bed.

Horatio guessed that once spoken, that word was the old man's passport to the undiscovered country. Leaving his fellow traveller alone in the empty chamber, he returned to his room to prepare for the final stage of his journey.

"Fate has no mercy. I mourn alone,
Telling myself the tale of my griefs.
There's no man alive to whom I may talk
Frankly of my fate, or confess my cares.
It's only too true that a man is wise
To trap his thoughts tight in his head,
And fasten his feelings firm in his breast.
A spent spirit can't fight fate.
Hard thoughts don't help. A secret is safe
If you keep the key secure in your skull.
So I, sorrow's servant, forlorn of my fatherland,
Fetter my feelings deep in my heart;
Ever since I, in a distant day
Gave to the ground my giver of gold,
The lord I loved. Then woeful as winter
I quit his cairn, and committed my keel
To the water's waste. Near and far
Through the world I searched, sick for a home,
Hungry for a hall: wanting only one
To befriend me, friendless, one wistful to wind me
In welcoming arms. So why in the world should I not
Despair, and my heart grow
Dark with the northern night sky's
Annunciation of snow, when I see
Peerless princes, royal retainers,
Such valiant men so suddenly vanish,
The homesteads vacated, voided the halls?
Between heaven and hell, this whole middle-earth
Moults and moulders, withers and wanes.

FROM THE WANDERER

7
At sea

W aking from a dream-haunted sleep, Horatio rose from the deck and, standing in the boat's prow, smelt on the seaward breeze the unmistakable odour of land. Behind him, a line of grey light delineated the eastern horizon. Ahead, somewhere in that mass of obscurity where sea and sky met and divided, he could distinctly sense the presence of his destination, that famous holy island that would soon rise from the sea in green, improbable isolation. There, he knew, among the pious brethren of the Lindisfarne community, he would find the object of his quest. The possible futures that might be extrapolated from that discovery had not yet fully shaped themselves in his mind. Sufficient unto the day: here, at least, the first part of his mission, after fifteen long years, would be accomplished.

Sails furled against a head wind, the boat was propelled on its course by the quiet, rhythmic motion of its oars. Waves slapped softly against the sharp keel, running with a flurry of feathery eddies along the sides of the hull, converging at the stern to form a foaming wake over which the gulls circled and screamed.

From the stern, the mellifluous voice of the *scop* kept time with the oars, beating out a rhythm in regular alliterative phrases. He was chanting one of the old English elegies, songs of heartbreak and separation that seemed, paradoxically, to console the mariners for their own homesickness, the temporary exile of their own long voyage.

Attuning his mind to the language and phrasing, Horatio could readily identify with the poem's stock situations and sentiments, as the singer sang of a life of exile, of a man condemned to an endless sea-voyage towards an unknown destination. He sang of one who had left behind him all worldly joy and all cheerful society, together with the beloved lord he had committed to the ground. Like the exile in the poem, Horatio too had his closely guarded secrets, locked tight in his skull; he too had found himself banished from the protection of his adopted lord, a wanderer on the face of the earth. He knew the sharp pangs of remembered pleasures and the bitterness of loss.

He too had felt the raven tips of despair's dark wing brush his face, and often regretted that he had not, when the opportunity offered itself, drained the poisoned cup and shared with his lord that grim last supper. And as the singer chanted his praises of patience and fortitude, his heart tightened with a firm sense of pride in the determined resolve with which he had pursued his vocation. But he also felt, listening again to the familiar lament for worldly transience, symbolised by the legendary devastation of the Great Flood, and marked by the desolate ruins of fallen civilisations like those of Greece and Rome, the irresistible magnetism of faith. For if human power and potentiality ultimately counted, in the *longue durée* of history, for so little, then in what power could a man place his trust but the service of that Lord whose kingdom endured for ever?

As the song closed, with its formal Christian coda, tears filled Horatio's eyes: bitter tears of regret, generous tears of acceptance and resignation.

> "Blessed the man
> Who hungers for grace; who longs
> For the love, and craves for the comfort
> Of the Father in heaven. All succour,
> All safety, all certainty, all love
> Lie only with Him, our only
> Assurance. He is our haven; He
> Is our home."

8

Holy Island

July 1065

The codex lay on the table, a stiff sheet of parchment serving as its cover, the sheets bound together at the right edge with a looped and knotted cord. Turning over the blank yellow frontispiece, the boy quickly scanned the neatly scripted page of contents. He recognised some of the titles, and realised that the leaves of English verse he had observed, a few days previously, in the *scriptorium,* had now been collated together with other documents into the text before him. It was an unusual occurrence for a book to be specially prepared for his perusal and the circumstance deepened his already whetted curiosity.

Even more unusual, he found, on turning the leaves, were the contents themselves. Although he had read widely and deeply in the monastery's library, the formal programme of reading imposed by his tutor was strictly controlled, consisting almost exclusively of divinity, grammar and rhetoric, and written exclusively in Latin and Greek. This discipline was strictly observed by Brother Caedmon, a monk of substantial learning and piety, who vigilantly policed the borders of the boy's curiosity. Here, though, was a collection of writings, mostly in English, more diversified than any he had previously been presented with: poems and songs, extracts from ancient sagas and legends, historical chronicles, riddles and charms.

On the other hand, the fact that Brother Caedmon had left him charged with explicit instruction to read the codex, was in itself more surprising than the fact of its existence. Though the intellectual environment of the monastery was preserved as one of absolute orthodoxy, the boy had derived from some of the brethren a distinct sense of attachment to writings not wholly in conformity with God's law and the doctrines of Holy Church. He had heard, on more than one occasion, one of the monks reciting from memory some old heroic poem celebrating the great deeds and memorable exploits of the old Danes and Norsemen. These performances were frowned upon and their originator soon censored into silence by the abbot; but not before the boy had caught through them imaginative glimpses of an older, vivid and exciting, pagan world.

Now he had been ordered to encounter that world directly. Caedmon had marked with torn strips of parchment several passages he was expected to digest before evening. Glancing through them he immediately apprehended that they all in some way related, either in history or legend, to the land of Denmark, the home he had never seen. As he read deeper into the codex, his initial curiosity solidified into a distinct conviction that the stories he was reading had something to do with himself.

The most substantial passage was a Latin chronicle, written by an emissary of the church, recounting the histories of the Danish and Norwegian kings. This he settled first to read and found in it nothing unusual. The broad outlines of the history were already familiar to him and he recognised in the writer's tone a characteristically inflexible orthodoxy that distorted everything it recorded:

> *For after this, Amled himself was slain in his own court by poison. So the wicked godless life of this king and his brother brought Amled to an ignominious death. Thus always is God's judgement dealt harshly to those who disobey his will. And while those who win earthly glory believe they can cheat God's vengeance, their success is granted only that their violent ends, unexpected, may be the more bitter and disappointing.*

The boy was already sophisticated enough in his reading to recognise how heavily overlaid with Christian orthodoxy was this narrative of his ancestral kings and princes. And as if to underline this context of appropriation, adjoining the chronicle was an Old English heroic lay celebrating the exploits of these same 'savage and unreclaimed' warriors of the north. It was a story he remembered having heard recited by one of the monks, the story of how King Amled of Denmark slew Fortenbrasse on the shores of Norway.

Amledsaga

Spear-Danes, hear! While I sing
A truthful tale from the dawn of days
Of a bitter battle on Grimstad strond:
Where a prince of the Norse, fierce Fortenbrasse
Bid to the fight, for freedom or blood,
The doer of deeds, Amled the Dane.

By the rime-cold sea, flowered with frost,
Dragon ships, shelved on the ice,
Hid the horde from the Norseman's lance.
Spears of the foe darkened the shore.

Then strode forth, firm in his pride,
Brave Fortenbrasse, and began his boast:
'Tarry, sea-farers, not long in this land,
Kingdom of kin by my fathers right:
Listen, and hear what the Norse-folk say.
Our long spears, our ancient swords,
Swords of our fathers, keen for your blood,
Thief of lands, robber of thrones.
Let Norsemen rule where Norse-folk dwell.
I Fortenbrasse, Anlaf's son,
Here claim my right where my father reigned.
Return now, Danes, to your Danish lands,
Your fertile fields, where your lives may be long.
Take back to the Danes your dragon-ships
Unburned, your bodies still unpierced
By the hungry points of our ice-cold spears.'

Amled, enraged at the Norseman's pride
Smote his axe, frosted with rime,
Sheer on the strond, splintering ice.
So that the Norseman might soon know
How fierce a heart he dared to the fight

In a voice of war, he weighed these words:
'See where my blade, battle-bright,
Scars this soil. So my sword
Will mark my power in wounds and pain.
Turn now, and hasten, back to your homes:
Or finish with words, and fall to the fight.'

The Danish horde drew their swords;
The Norsemen grasped their lances fast.
The shining air shivered with fear.
Then Fortenbrasse, angry in turn,
A tempest of words tossed back to the king:
'Think you to win with boastful speech
The land we Norsemen nursed with blood?
Prove your title, two-crowned king;
Stand for your right against my shield.
Let single fight, foe against foe,
Decide the victor: do you dare
Dane, live or die by a Norseman's sword?

Amled raised high his hawk-hung wrist:
And towards the foe let his falcon fly.
Shouldering shield, he hefted axe,
Fearless and firm, and strode to the fight.
Brave Fortenbrasse swung his sword
Stiff and stern he stood to the foe.
As when a dragon-ship driven to north
By whirling winds off Iceland's strond,
Blown by the blast through boiling seas
Clashes its keel on a cunning rock,
Shatters its prow in splintering shafts:
So Fortenbrasse, roused by wrath,
Flailed with his sword at Amled's helm,
Fell with shock on the Danish shield.
Amled's axe, heft to the height,
With thunderous force fell on the foe.
Split to the breasts fell Fortenbrasse;
His spirit fled from the snow-cold shore.

High his hand the hero raised
Hoisted his triumph above his head;

Low the foe lay at his feet,
His vanity mastered, vanquished his might.
So the Lord smiled on Amled his servant
Gave him the day for the deeds of his life:
Punished the proud man with pains of death.

Beasts die, kinsmen die:
    Man is mortal.
But a good man's name
    Lives for ever.
Beasts die, kinsmen die:
    Man is mortal.
But one thing lives:
    The fame of a great deed.

The boy read on and on into the manuscript, his imagination fired by stories of gods and monsters, heroes and villains. Much of it he found puzzling, all of it strange. Yet he could not shake off a conviction of familiarity with that which he had never seen before. Somewhere in here were clues that led to the secret of his identity and origin: but he could not find them. Some passages stirred him with emotions he had never felt until now. He was reading of the death of Baldr, and feeling as he read of the god's funeral an overwhelming sense of bereavement and loss.

Weeping, the gods gently carried the body of Baldr down to the sea's edge. There, riding at anchor, lay his ship Hringhorni, the most magnificent of all vessels. On the deck they built Baldr's pyre, and there they committed to the flames the corpse of their beloved, together with his horse and his treasures. When Baldr's wife Gerda saw the funeral preparations, straightway her heart broke with grief, and she too was laid on the fire beside her husband. With a single blow from his great hammer, Thor sent the burning ship gliding over the surface of the world ...

With the bang of an iron latch, the heavy door suddenly opened. The boy turned quickly, startled by the intrusion, still rapt in the absorbed anticipation of his reading. It was only Brother Caedmon. But as the monk entered, the boy became aware of another man who stood behind him: a lean figure, tall enough to have to stoop under the lintel, folded in a rough travelling cloak. The boy was aware of a strong, thin, sunburnt face, skin wrinkled with travel and exposure, intelligent grey eyes, fair hair cut short in an almost priestly fashion. Brother Caedmon stepped modestly aside to allow the stranger to precede, thus informing the boy that the newcomer was a Freeman. The boy returned the traveller's courteous bow, his wonder intensifying. He had met many such strangers, and was too well-schooled in courtesy to be in any way over awed by such an encounter. But the look on the stranger's face perplexed him in the extreme. It was a look neither of friendliness or hostility, neither of respect nor contempt. It was, inexplicably, a look of recognition.

My Father. Methinks I see my Father.

Part four

Holy Island

'D o you know who I am?' was the traveller's initial question.

The boy shook his head. They were seated facing one another across the wooden table in the same chamber and Horatio was filling his eyes with the object of his quest. So long lost, from the moment of his birth; fatherless and motherless; now found, re-discovered by an ever wakeful providence aiming at purposes beyond the reach of his innocent imagination.

'My name is Horatio. I am from Denmark, across the sea, which you know as your native land. I knew both your father, and your mother'.

The boy's face continued to remain unchanged as Horatio's incredible story unfolded. For it had not needed these outlandish words, kindly and courteously spoken by a man towards whom he instinctively warmed in a voluntary motion of trust, to inform the boy that his past contained some inscrutable secret. Just as Horatio had recognised him by an uncanny resemblance to his dead father, so the boy himself had, for a passing moment, glimpsed Horatio through the eyes of another's knowledge, apprehended his appearance through the spirit of some departed love. He knew, before Horatio spoke a word, that this man carried with him the secret that would open the tomb of memory, unlock the sealed archive of his past.

Now, as he listened, struck at one level by the incredulity of the tale, he was aware, at some deeper stratum of his being, that this was indeed his own forgotten and remembered story. Horatio explained that his father and mother were both dead, though in the country of his birth they were remembered, by some, as the wisest prince, and the fairest lady, in their own, or in any other kingdom. He told the boy that he was the son of Prince Hamlet, a prince who should have been a king, if justice, rather than wickedness, had been permitted to prevail.

'I know you have read of your father. From the histories you will know of Prince Hamlet as he who went mad, and murdered both his uncle and his mother'

But none of this, Horatio assured him, was true. Such tales were the slanderous rumours spread abroad by those who took power on the king's death, and wanted to discredit their predecessors in the throne of Denmark. For it had been Hamlet's wicked uncle Claudius who had murdered both his brother King Amled, and his consort Queen Gertrude, and who had finally been the occasion of his own father's brutal slaughter.

Then he took from a dusty travelling-satchel an embossed leather folder, bearing the royal arms of Denmark, which he placed on the table before the boy.

'Here you will find your father's story. The brothers have taught you Greek, they tell me. Do you read it with fluency and confidence?' The boy nodded assent. 'Then you will need no help from me. Read your father's own testimony, in his own words as I have faithfully translated them. This is his journal, containing all his thoughts and feelings as he committed them to private record. Here you will find expounded your father's own mind; and here you will find, in the other documents, proofs of the murderous manner of his unhappy death. When you have read what is there, you will understand whose son you are, and know what you must do'.

Gently Horatio lifted the cover of the folder to reveal the initial page of neatly scripted Greek uncials. Then he left his seat, and moved over to the arched window that gave onto a prospect of the sea. He leaned against the embrasure and looked across the blue distance towards the east. The boy began to read.

Hamlet's Tables

To my son Hamlet against his setting forth for school in Wittenberg, in this year of Grace 1049. This book to be the repository of his acquired wisdom and knowledge.

May the Lord watch between thee and me while we are absent the one from the other.

AMLED OF DANMARK

With the best of intentions hath my noble father bestowed upon me this notebook, which is to be, as such volumes are designed to be in this lettered age, as the very mirror of my mind, a surface that may take record of all forms and pressures that youth and observation may copy there. Every young fop nowadays carries about with him his 'tables', and is ostentatious in scribbling whenever he pretends to have heard a wise word, or finds some passionate impulse urging its way into verse.

Yet, if only to please my father, I will endeavour to keep this diary when I embark on my travels, both those upon the surface of the earth, and those through the uncharted waters of the mind. Why, these jottings could one day become a book, expounding all my opinions on kingship, government, the right and the good – *The Education of a Prince*, perhaps? By means of such a text I might hope to persuade some of my neighbour kings to desist from butchery and lust, and to adopt good manners, piety and the delights of knowledge.

Resolve then, Hamlet, to observe this discipline – by the end of each day to have entered onto these pages something of wisdom, truth or experience.

22 December 1049
Helsingor

So! By my noble father's bidding, I am after all to join Horatio in Wittenberg, immediately following the season wherein our Saviour's birth is celebrated. I had hopes, growing to such an advancement in years with no tutor but my fancy, and no school but my father's library, to live out my days in as pleasurable an ignorance as any ploughboy. For what needs a Dane to be taught but to drink deep and cry 'God save the king'? To sink a tankard or to raise an axe?

And what of my poor dear Ofelia? How will she brook the sudden and protracted absence of her prince? How indeed will I fare without her? How may I sustain the even temporary loss of that heavenly face, wherein one may read strange matter; those eyes whose glance has inscribed such deep and lasting messages within the book and volume of my brain?

Well, Horatio (my forward companion whose work I shamelessly cribbed as a schoolboy) and I are to be re-united as fellow-students in the University where I will hope to derive from his mental advancement something of the like benefit. It is for him to wean me from idleness to scholarship, from love to learning; to conduct my tastes from Ovid to Aristotle, Catullus to Plato. To that sophisticated traveller, it falls to rub the rough edges off a crude Norseman's wit and to polish me up fit for presentation to the doctors of the University.

Even now I am half-minded to plead for reversal of my father's hard-won consent that he may instead let me enlist in the army currently mustering to attack the English. Who would not, when all is said, rather be a man of action than a scholar, a thick-limbed hero than a pale, peeled monk? Examples gross as earth exhort us. Witness this army of such mass and charge, led by a delicate and tender prince – the great Fortinbras, whose fearsome reputation will set you straight a-trembling, and whose name alone is sufficient to open a man's bowels (or a maid's legs) – whose spirit, with divine ambition puffed, makes mouths at the invisible event, exposing what is mortal and unsure to all that fortune, death and danger dare – even for an egg-shell! Why, such a one as he would find a quarrel in a straw, when honour's at the stake.

As I pack my books of philosophy and logic, my Ramus and my Scotus, my Ethics and my Analytics, I glance through my window at such post-haste and rummage of military preparation; and see, to my shame, the imminent death of twenty thousand men, that for a fantasy and trick of fame go to their graves like beds; fighting for a plot no bigger than a grave, not large enough to hide the slain!

But lie thou there, my sword; let me for once be deaf

to the summons of the battle-horn. Harder struggles await me than these pitiable and petty squabbles. I mean, in all seriousness, when my great father embarks for the fields of Valhalla, to rule in Denmark as a new kind of king. At the University I seek the knowledge that will enable me, in due season, to accomplish this ambition.

23 December 1049
Helsingor

My lady Ofelia writes me that she may not meet me today as promised and I must needs take her letter as poor substitute for her company. It appears that she received yesterday, from her father who is absent in Norway on the king my father's business, such a communication as she thought never to receive, and hopes never to receive again.

Therein, she advises me, her loving father, careful I doubt not only for her safety and protection, tells her in the roundest terms that he is acquainted with our mutual affection; that she should believe nothing of my professions of love and trust nothing in our courtship. He warns her to break off our correspondence and no more to entertain talk or society with myself.

Polonius must not long labour under these misapprehensions, believing as he plainly does that I mean to make his daughter not my wife and princess, but my whore. Though it will, indeed, be a hard task to persuade my dear father-in-law-in-prospect, as I now should style him, that he is mistaken, so dearly is he attached to his own words and ideas. For a mere maid to challenge her father's judgement, Ofelia must needs be ready to defend her love, as the bravest of knights, against all comers. Yet notwithstanding her firmness of resolve and bravery of spirit, I cannot permit her do this alone. I must stand with her in this trial, and make known to the world the truth of our virtuous love, and everlasting pledge of mutual faith.

My sweet lady cannot be more solicitous than I am myself to have our love declared. Though for the lascivi- ous, secrecy may be an incitement to lust – no time so well-suited to illicit passion than the protective shadows of deep midnight – with our love it is far otherwise. A love that hopes only for lawful wedlock, by its nature seeks the light of day, and longs to breathe the blessed air, to feel the healing touch of the sovereign sun. Until our reciprocal affection be admitted to the world, we cannot choose but remain wrongly burdened by the secret shame that belongs to guilty passion and adulter- ous lust.

I have this very day spoken with my lady the Queen and fully confided to her all the circumstance of my posi- tion. She, like the loving mother and trusting soul she is, has naught but praise for Ofelia, kind wishes for me and copious blessings to bestow upon our union. What daughter could ever hope to gain, not only a second mother after loss of the first, but one whose maternal tenderness looks to exceed even the fast affections of she who first groaned my love to deliver!

It is now incumbent on my good mother to address our suit unto my noble father the king. For he, she tells me, has been revolving for no little time some notion of my attachment to a foreign princess, in a marriage made, not in heaven, but in the council chamber; a union instituted for the mutual comfort of nations and for the procreation of treaties. Let the good councillors dispute as they may and howe'er she may be the fairest and purest of all ladies, I'll none of it.

Yet is my great father of unshakeable opinion in matters of state. To him, as to all the noblemen of his generation, in point of marriage a woman may be weighed in
kingdoms, and valued in principalities. The men of the
old times had many wives, or none, and allowed no
woman to interfere with their battle-plans or curtail
their carouses. And certain it is that my dear father does
but grudgingly accept the Word of Our Lord, and the
wisdom of Holy Church. He, I know, would of his own
opinion give no countenance to a love-match; for he
would see no let or hindrance to our mutual pleasures,
notwithstanding what woman sleeps in the king's bed
and bears his children.

Yet I doubt nothing that my dear mother will so prevail upon him as to overcome these ignoble and unchris-
tian ambitions. For despite himself, he has long loved her
as faithfully and truly as any Christian husband ought to
cherish his wife. Why it is long since, and well before the
weaknesses of age began to curb the appetite, that he
willingly forsook the embraces of those many women tra-
ditionally approved as fitting companions for a king's
bed. Though it is no solace to me that I lack siblings, yet
am I distinguished among the princes of my generation
in that there are no little imitations of my father, got on
the wrong side of the blanket, filling the corridors of
Helsingor. For my father, there has been but one woman,
one he has so dearly cherished that he might not beteem
the winds of heaven visit her face too roughly. Why, he
would hang upon her, as if increase of appetite did grow
by what it feeds on!

Both I and my lady must school ourselves to patience,
and let our love be presented to my father through the
mirror of that kindred affection he bears my mother.
I have urged the queen to seek audience with my father

ere this week be out; for at midnight on the Sabbath
following I am appointed to embark on my journey. The
king being much busied with matters of state, she will
need some womanly wiles if she is to obtain from him a
proper degree of attention. But if she cannot obtain this
suit, then there is none that can.

28 December 1049
At sea

I am en route for Wittenberg. My mother could gain no
audience with the king, despite her best endeavours,
good woman, to broach the subject of my affections.
Once he has successfully concluded his present negotia-
tions with the Swede, she will present my suit to him.

It is but a short space, but two months – nay, not so
much, not two. On my return to Denmark for the festival
of *Eostre*[*], I look to meet my Ofelia not as my secret
inamorata but as she will then be known in the eyes of
Denmark and of the world, as my beloved, my wife, my
queen. So now to sleep: we make port at Lubeck in the
morning and begin our overland journey into Germany.
Rest you peacefully, sweet Ofelia. Would you were here at
my side, or I there at yours.

1 January 1050
Near Hamburg

In sooth the fast-resolved discipline I enjoined upon
myself at the outset of this journal is thoroughly
breached before I had established for it any habit of
observance! How I underestimated the hardships of
travel, and the weariness induced by a plodding nag's

[*] Easter

progress across this flat and dreary land. Why, surely this is a piece of the firmament that God first created out of the void of waste and water! On every hand the plains stretch as far as the eye can see, all of the same colourless hue of muddy earth. Somewhere in the distance the land meets a low leaden sky as neutral as the ground. And the cold! Raw and rotten, cutting at the bones through clothes, skin and flesh. Occasionally we pass a settlement along the road, mud huts, a few skinny beasts, untethered, that huddle close only because there is nowhere else for them to go, and peasants filthy in their poverty and rags. How painfully already I miss the mountains and the sea, the ever-changing clouds mirrored in the sparkling fjord, the clean wooden huts and neat stone churches! Though I thought to be engaged in a journey from barbarism to civilisation, I find myself instead travelling deeper into a dark night of bestial deprivation. What would I not give to hear again the mountain winds stirring the pine-tops, to breathe again that cold, clean air, heaven's own breath!

Yet one cannot help but pity these poor creatures, especially the women and children, who stare defiantly at strangers out of their hovels, too oppressed to rob, too proud to beg. But their eyes flare at you from out the shadows of their rags, and with a fierce courage of desperation, they stare you out of countenance. Were I the Elector, I would set no store by the loyalty of these people, who have so little to lose that they would fear nothing in any attempt to gain more than the little they have.

Tonight we are camped some leagues from Hamburg. The town is away to the west and out of our way, or I would urge my fellows to seek its shelter and some prospect of warmth and fellowship. Tomorrow we pick

up the route of the River Elbe and rendezvous with men
of the Elector's who have it in charge to provide some
barge that will take us up the river to Wittenberg. The
deck of a boat appears in my imagination as welcoming
as my mother's breast, by comparison with this horse's
back, the rough hide of which has become to me a sorely
troublesome old acquaintance.

I commend my father, my mother and my dear Ofelia
to God's keeping.

(With every league I journey from Denmark, the face
of my fair Ofelia grows in my mind's eye more distinct,
the sense of her presence ever more close and real. God
guard her, and bring me with all speed back to her arms).

10 January 1050
Wittenberg

Today we arrived in Wittenberg after a slow passage
along the Elbe, on a barge drawn by oxen – a picturesque,
if primitive, mode of transportation. At midday we
reached the town which is strung out all along the banks
of the stream. The river-front is cut and carved into little
basins, each separated ingeniously by a platform for
boarding and loading, where boats may be moored. The
river also serves as a natural moat to protect the town's
unfortified buildings from a frontal assault. From the
centre of the town a bridge thrusts out and, spanning
the river, is closed by a portcullis at the town end.

The town is indeed very pretty, a jumble of houses all
facing different ways, some with steep roofs, some with
shallow; some red-tiled, some yellow-straw-thatched. At
one end of the town stands the *Schlosskirche*,[*] an elegant

---

[*] castle-church

building with a graceful tower, tall arched windows between beautifully proportioned buttresses, the whole resting at the foot of a wooded hill. Surmounting the red tiled roof is a little spire, a miniature copy of that which tops the tall round tower. As its name suggests, this is both castle and church: a fine deep ditch surrounds it with well-guarded footbridges providing access to its doors. At the other end of the town, only a walk away, is the college, with its adjoining monastery, where I will be staying, and where this forenoon I hope to greet Horatio.

(Later)

Why, this Wittenberg is as fine a place as any I could have imagined. It is not so much a university in a town, as a town turned university. The college, the church and the monastery so dominate as to render the whole place a tiny city of light and learning. It is a humming hive of studious diligence, pious devotion and charitable work. Everywhere the cadent melodies of many bells call to labour, to devotion, to scholarly exercise. If the bells for a moment cease, the air softly reverberates with an after-hum, like a struck tuning-fork, until soon, you can be sure, some other peal will take up the music again.

Everything here in Wittenberg revolves around college and church. The townspeople either labour for the abbot, work in service to the university, or trade goods and produce to both. Thus the town is there to serve these houses of piety and learning, and not the other way around. Here students walk the streets in their gay fluttering livery: they talk and laugh, drink in the ale-houses, sup at the inns. I have never witnessed in any place such an atmosphere of liberty. Above all strange is the confidence bred of a guaranteed freedom from the anxiety of attack. One reason for this enviable liberty must be, I cannot fail to remind myself, that here we are so deep inland as to be safe from the depredations of my own people, the notorious pirates of the north. Of course, though no sea-raiders would penetrate this far, there are not wanting land-raiders; and in a situation of war the town could easily be besieged. But here war seems an unusual occurrence, rather than, as it is in my own kingdom, a condition of existence.

This afternoon, with my old friend and much-loved companion, Horatio, I sauntered the streets, drinking in greedily this strange air of peace and stability, this atmosphere in which true thought and honest devotion become possible, nay are even actively encouraged. Horatio, the best of guides, introduced me to some of his newfound companions; mainly German youths of noble rank, but including some more exotic foreign students – Romans from the south, a Greek from Alexandria, even a prince of Muscovy. They seem, in their every word and motion, so alive with knowledge, and yet they wear their culture so lightly and easily. How unlike the young men of my own race who seem now, by contrast, as thick-headed as oxen: their tastes low, their conversation dull; even their courtesy clumsily imitated from the out-dated fashions of an old Frankish ambassador!

These youths in Wittenberg truly belong to a different world and their society provides, for me, a glimpse of what a new Denmark could become under my rule. A land of peace and amity, dedicated to the pursuits of piety and learning, free from fear of the sword. A land where every man, woman and child would be equally entitled to love and liberty, and to the means of existence. A land where each man might love his neighbour as himself. What a dream! Yet why should not King Hamlet bring it one day to realisation?

11 January 1050
Monastery of St Augustine, Wittenberg

Myself and my fellow-pupils being up betimes this morning, since no sluggishness is tolerated here, and the tasks
of the long day and evening already imposed, this is
likely to be my only opportunity of making an entry in
my journal. So much is occurring, with such rapidity,
meshing my mind and spirit in a whirl of sensations and
impressions. New experience, new ideas, new possibilities. The need to set down, in some reasonable order, my
first perceptions of Wittenberg, is become of pressing
urgency. So I have seized the opportunity of a brief remis-
sion, while the brothers are at their devotions, to
attempt a summary, albeit premature, of my education
thus far.

I write cramped into the window-seat of my tiny chamber, a garret room high up under the eaves of the Augustinian monastery. It is a tall house, three stories high, its
frontage divided by elegantly proportioned windows, and
surrounded by extensive gardens that slope away towards
the Elbe. My room, like those of all my fellow-scholars,
affords space only for sleep and prayer. 'Tis a chastening
experience, for some of my companions as for me, to be
treated, from the outset, no differently from any other
poor threadbare scholar. Here there are no privileges
attaching to rank, no enlarged liberty extended to
wealth. We are here, our surroundings continually
remind us, to read and study, think and pray; to speak
and to listen, to ponder and to learn. The only rewards
attainable within such a strait regimen are those of
wisdom and grace. Here no man is flattered for his ances-
try, or valued for his family's name. Praise is bestowed,
and that sparingly, only on those who by diligence

earn their commendations.

Despite these cramped conditions, one would not indeed wish to be accommodated elsewhere in the monastery. A apart from the fact that abstinence from luxury is the norm throughout this community (the larger chambers below are communal dormitories), these little roof-top eyries, where we scholars nest, afford the most wonderful views over Wittenberg. Crouched into the seat of my white-framed dormer window, I look out over the monastery's neatly-landscaped gardens which lie, this bright, cold morning, powered with frost; across a ramshackle tumble of red and blue roof-tops, of all shapes and sizes and angles of elevation; to the river, sparkling in the winter sunlight, and dotted all over with the little coloured sails of vessels that ply their restless trade, up and down the stream. Across the Elbe, rich green meadows, providing fodder for many a slow-grazing fat beast, extend widely to the north, gradually breaking into scrubby undergrowth, and merging eventually into a dark line of woodland. Beyond the forest, the horizon lifts into gentle contours to reveal the slopes of blue, wooded hills.

I have already hinted that here, rising is intolerably early. Through what seemed to me an impenetrable darkness, a cacophony of bells clanged every sleeper harshly awake. Notwithstanding our difficulties in rising and dressing in darkness, by the time the merciless bells had ceased their clangour, we were all obediently seated at our benches, faces scrubbed clean like so many schoolboys, awaiting the arrival of our first lecturer, Brother Martin. Having been all my life familiar with our Augustinian brethren in Denmark, I had neither any particular fear of subjection to an intimidating discipline, nor any sanguine expectation of encountering great and adventurous minds. In he came, as prompt as we, modest and unassuming, of middling height, nondescript in his white Augustinian habit, eyes downcast and bald tonsured scalp shining, muttering under his breath inaudible prayers. He bid us good morning with as much humility as one finds in the most servile of his brotherhood, his voice soft in tone, though sharp in enunciation.

But then, when he raised his eyes to look at us, flaming with a fierceness of conviction, they were the eyes of an archangel. Though his voice was soft, when he called on the Lord for the gift of grace to be bestowed on our poor understandings, his words seemed to me like the voice that Ezekiel heard in his vision, when the doorposts of the temple moved at the sound.

Then oh, how ill-prepared I found myself (though as well-prepared as I could be by what passes among us Danes as a liberal education) for the dizzying revelations of genuine learning! I count myself as well-trained as any in Logic and Rhetoric, Grammar and Philosophy; for, after all, the monks who taught me these disciplines at Helsingor, learned their craft in just such seats of learning as this. But who would have guessed at the ferment of new ideas that has been bubbling away under the surface of our lives; or how far the best minds have travelled while we barbarians of the far north have complacently accepted the learning of twenty years before!

From my very earliest memories, I have always been able to win any argument, and vanquish any intellectual opponent, by unscrupulous use of the tools of Logic and Rhetoric. Even my father's chief ministers would retreat in haste as soon as I mentioned Aristotle's *Analytics*, or began to deploy the formulae and propositions categorised in the *Sumulae logicales* of Petrus Hispanus. Human knowledge, I have always firmly believed, rests on verifiable experience. What can we possibly claim to *know*, other than that we can see and touch, hear and smell and taste? The things we know are facts, and facts exist in and by themselves, not as parts of some unverifiable universal. Generalisations are names we give to collections of facts, and we understand the relations between facts by logic.

Divine knowledge, my learning has always told me, is not properly knowledge at all: we cannot know God in the same way as we know our bodies and our surroundings. Theology is not accessible to rational thought. What can we know of God's will, save that which is embodied in the traditions of the church? And is there not enough to concern us here in this life, as we strive to understand the nature of things, and to bring them into conformity with the divine will, without wasting our time on useless speculation as to the nature of the unknowable?

Now these beliefs lie in smoking ruins, burnt to ashes by the searing lightning of Brother Martin's intellect. It is said that he became a monk, as St Paul became a Christian, when God threw him to the ground with the help of a thunderbolt. Certain it is that he has unhorsed my faith in reason and science, right here at the very beginning of this long Damascus road. He teaches that we can indeed know God, and attain an understanding of God's will, by reading the Scriptures. The will of God is absolute, imperative, and renders all our scholastic efforts to classify and categorise reality, superfluous. The mind of man is as weak and corrupt as his body: he can in turn know nothing save that which divine grace permits him to know. Man's thoughts, his achievements, his works are of no value to God unless God chooses to confer value on them through grace.

His text was St Paul's *Epistle to the Romans* (from my

recollection, a text dealing with old and unintelligible controversies). But he spoke of it in ways that caused me to wonder whether I had ever truly read it. My notes are fragmentary, but should capture the argument:

"The sum and substance of this Epistle, argues Brother Martin, "is to eliminate all the righteousness of the flesh and to magnify sin and nothingness, so that finally Christ and his righteousness may enter us in place of the things we have wiped out.

"In God's presence man does not become just by doing just works. By *being* just, he does just deeds.

"Why does man take pride in his works, which do not please God because they have merit, but only because they are works of the faith that can alone please Him? There is no good works but the search for grace.

"The sinner cannot save himself, and cannot be saved by his own exertions; but only by grace conferred from without:

"Not that which comes from ourselves. But that which comes from without into us.

"Not that which rises from the earth. But that which comes down from heaven."

Hardly glancing up to measure the effect of his words, Brother Martin collected his papers and left us, his parting gift a set of aphorisms that puzzle and bewilder, echo and intrigue.

Now before tomorrow's lecture I am to read the *Epistle to the Galatians* and so must, for the time being, bid farewell to my journal.

15 January 1050
Wittenberg

"The just shall live by faith" (*Romans*, 1.17). Indeed, but what follows? Granted that, being fallen, we are so

depraved that even our good works cannot satisfy God.
We are saved only by faith in the redeeming merits of
Christ, whose sacrifice on the Cross alone has the power
to take away sin. The faith which enables us to attain this
redemption is God's gift. We live by faith alone, by a sure
and constant trust in the divine mercy promised in
Christ.

What need, then, for Confession? What value can be
attributed to the sacrament of Penance, and to priestly
Absolution? The church offers, through the sale of indul-
gences, to free us from the penalty of sin: yet we know
there is no protection from God's judgement, except
through faith. We pray for the saints to intercede with
God to help us, or to shorten a late loved one's passage
through purgatory. Yet how can any of this please God,
who alone both judges and absolves? We have blindly
accepted the authority of a church that in truth seems
founded on false promises, and that knows nothing of
how men may be justified with God.

Only think what consequences follow from these
truths! If the church in some way stands between God
and man, and the church errs, then how is man to come
directly to relationship with God, if not through the
church? What of the kings who accept the authority of
the church and of the Pope? For it is not, I see now, by
obedience to the church that we are saved, but by obedience to God. Why, some of my German companions tell
me that even the church's entitlement to property is
questioned by some of these bold 'reformers'. Why, they
ask, may not a Christian prince be the head of his own
Church, *fidei defensor,** and the clergy his spiritual counsellors? So that he who has power over the poor wretched

---

* Defender of the faith

bodies of his subjects, may also by grace undertake the cure of their souls? Dangerous, but thrilling speculations, that would be of great interest to some of my cleverer countrymen. With a tenth of the wealth of the church in Denmark, I could build a hundred universities throughout my dominions ...

Well, for this evening at least I am glad for a while to put aside theology and politics, and to give some rest to my over-exercised brain. For tonight the Elector holds an accustomed feast in the *Schlosskirche*, to which we scholars are invited, that we may enjoy some brief but welcome respite from our lives of abstinence and privation. Horatio tells me that a company of players, the same I have seen perform in my father's court at Helsingor, are to play before the Elector and his guests a tragedy. I hope it may not be dull. Though I have seen these same rogues fill a hall with helpless laughter at their farcing and horseplay, when performing under the humourless eye of the Abbott, their antics may prove altogether more restrained.

16 January 1050
Wittenberg

Why, what an error was I in to doubt the talents of my old friends the tragedians! It seems that the low comedy and dull rhetoric I have heard from them at home, is merely the poor fodder they serve up for the raw appetites of the barbarian north (and I do confess, that when they played Seneca before my dear father, he slept soundly enough to discourage even the most versatile thespian). Tonight their playing was masterly, drama such as I have never seen performed. The play, never before acted, was excellent; well-digested in the scenes, set down with as much modesty as cunning. One clever

fellow opined that there were no sallets in the lines to
make the matter savoury, nor no matter in the phrase
that might indict the author of affectation. I can affirm
myself that the play was penned by an honest method, as
wholesome as it was sweet. Their theme was nothing less
than the Fall of Troy, finely adapted into good Saxon
verse from Virgil. The narrative, spoken by their chief
player in a voice of passing beauty and great force, would
by itself have held me spellbound. But these fellows, with
great invention and unparalleled skill, found means of
suiting the word to the action, the action to the word,
whereby Aeneas' tale to Dido unfolded before our very
eyes.

See, a dozen of these players, backs bent and arms
linked, a blanket thrown over their backs and a hobby-
horse thrust out in front, made themselves into as true a
Trojan horse as ever envisaged. Why, when Laocoon
stands up and hurls me a great spear into its chest, I
know not with what skill one of the fellows inside
caught and held it fast, nor how he contrived to 'scape
injury. Then, as the Trojans doused their torches and
took to their beds, off goes the horse's clout, and forth
comes a phalanx of Greek warriors, fully armed!

When this same spear-throwing priest stands to
sacrifice his bull (a squealing and lowing boy) to great
Neptunus, forth from beneath a table come sliding two
little fellows, as sinuous as any serpents, and clutch onto
Laocoon's arms, whence, on his efforts to shake 'em off,
they jerk and dangle like little crocodiles fastened onto
their prey. Then round his body they wrapped themselves, wriggling and hissing like very snakes, dragging
him down and choking out his life.

But oh, for heart-stopping tragedy no scene can compare with that wherein these fellows presented the death

of Priam. In the doorway the players had cleverly set a
false door, and through it comes bursting, with a splintering crash, great Pyrrhus' axe. My good Horatio, seeing
the blood drain from the countenances of some of our
companions, reassured them that this commotion must
needs be in jest, seeing that there were but two Northmen in Wittenberg, and neither of us was armed. But
there stands Pyrrhus, black as night in his sable armour,
his face hidden by a visor, great axe raised for slaughter.
Poor little Polites runs against him but pitilessly Pyrrhus
strikes him down. Then out runs old Priam, fumbling
with his rusty armour, a toothless Hecuba hanging on his
arm and seeking to restrain him; when with a fine
expression of tenderness and terror, he sees the body of
his murdered boy. Pyrrhus fends away with his bronze
shield a feeble thrust from the old man's spear; then
seizes the king by his snow-white hairs, drags him to the
altar, and raises on high his merciless axe. There, in my
mind's eye it still hangs, poised and suspended, and
there I fear will hang always. Certain it is, that throughout this terrible moment, not a breath escaped our
mouths, not an eye that did not contain behind its lashes
a caged tear. I confess that when his weapon fell, my eyes
closed against the dreadful sight. Strangely I pictured to
myself my own dear father; thinking perhaps, as does
Aeneas, that he and Priam were of an age ...

I begged from my friend, the principal player, his manuscript, so I could copy and get by heart the speeches
that accompanied this tragic show. Here I'll set it down:
it begins with Virgil's '*Vestibulum ante ipsum primoque in
limine Pyrrhus*':

> 'The rugged Pyrrhus – he whose sable arms
> Black as his purpose, did the night resemble ...'

I must break off: I am called to the inn to meet some

fellows who bring news from Denmark. What dreadful
summons can drag men from their beds at this time of
night, I know not.

March 1050
Helsingor

To be, or not to be? That is the question
  O that this too, too sullied flesh would melt! Thaw,
and resolve itself into a dew! Or that the Everlasting had
not fixed his canon 'gainst self-slaughter! That it should
come thus! But two months dead (nay, not so much, not
two): so excellent a king, that was, to this, Hyperion to a
satyr – heaven and earth! Must I remember?
  My father was a man, take him for all in all: I shall not
look upon his like again. What a piece of work is a man!
How noble in reason, how infinite in faculty; in form and
moving, how express and admirable; in action, how like
an angel; in apprehension, how like a god! The beauty of
the world, the paragon of animals! And yet, to me, what
is this quintessence of dust? Man delights not me – no,
nor woman neither.
  Indeed it goes so heavily with my disposition that this
goodly frame, the earth, seems to me a sterile promontory; this most excellent canopy, the air, this brave o'er-
hanging firmament, this majestical roof fretted with
golden fire – why, it appeareth nothing to me but a foul
and pestilent congregation of vapours. How weary, stale,
flat and unprofitable seem to me all the uses of this
world! Fie on't! Fie! 'Tis an unweeded garden that grows
to seed; things rank and gross in nature possess it
merely.
  To be, or not to be? Aye. There's the point.

March 1050
Helsingor

This day Horatio visits me, having heard I was not to be
permitted, by the will of my new sovereign, to return to
Wittenberg. He has spoken with some of his acquaintance among the young lords of the castle guard, and
brings me, from them, a strange tale indeed. They aver
they have seen, at midnight, my father's spirit, in arms,
here on the battlements. All is not well. I doubt some
foul play. Would the night were come!

ONE MAY SMILE, AND SMILE, AND BE A VILLAIN!

At least, I am sure it may be so in Denmark.
Oh, my prophetic soul! The serpent that did sting my
father's life, now wears his crown. So, uncle, there you
are.

Remember thee? Ay, thou poor ghost, while memory
holds a seat in this distracted globe. Remember thee?
Yea, from the table of my memory, I'll wipe away all trivial fond records; all saws of books, all forms, all pressures
past: and thy commandment all alone shall live, within
this book and volume of my brain, unmix'd with baser
matter. Oh, villain! villain! villain! smiling, damned villain!
Now to my word; it is 'Adieu, adieu; remember me'. O,
vengeance!

June 1050
Helsingor

I had almost forgot, these last few months, my faithful
tables; and greet their ever receptive pages, that have
taken all my confessions without imposing any

corresponding penance, again now with some feeling, I know not what, of valediction. For in truth, all's ill about my heart.

But does it not stand me now upon, to take revenge on this unnatural uncle? He, that hath killed my king, and whored my mother; popp'd in between the election and my hopes; set spies on me, and made me murderer? He that strewed mistrust between my poor Ofelia and me, made me wrong her, and was th' occasion of her death; he that conspired with the rebel Laertes, and with our ancient enemy the Polack, to put out an angle for my proper life? Is 't not perfect conscience, now, to quit him with this arm? And is't not to be damned to let this canker of our nature come in further evil?

To my ever-faithful friend Horatio, I will commit this book. To my loving and merciful Lord Jesus, I commit my soul. There is a special providence in the fall of a sparrow. If it be not now, it is to come. If it be not to come, it will be now. The readiness is all.

As the boy turned the last page of Hamlet's journal, he uncovered a number of letters, pinned together by a thin bright thread of gold wire. They were all addressed to his mother Ofelia, and had been seized by Horatio from where they had lain in the dead Queen's bosom.

Prince Hamlet to the Lady Ofelia
June 1049

To the celestial, and my soul's idol, the most beautified Ofelia. In that sweet name I name both my sovereign and my tormentor. To plead for her pity, her humble subject begs that she may place thus, in her excellent white bosom, these trifling but heartfelt verses, penned by one whose gift of eloquence comes nowhere near the lofty height of his subject:

> Doubt thou the stars are fire,
> Doubt that the sun doth move,
> Doubt truth to be a liar
> But never doubt I love.

O dear Ofelia, I am ill at these numbers, I have not art to reckon my groans, but that I love thee best, O most best, believe it; Adieu.

HAMLET

The Lord Laertes to the Lady Ofelia
June 1049

Dear sister: I write to you from a traveller's inn not many miles from Paris. There is little to report in the way of diverting traveller's tales since we have seen no place worthy the description, and person worth recognition.

My reason for writing to you so soon after my departure is however, of quite another kind. Though my straitened leisure allowed me before my departure only to broach the subject, I was unable, especially in the presence of our dear father, to open my heart as fully as I would to you touching the Lord Hamlet, and his apparent affection towards you. Though I count myself his friend, and have indeed sought to incite in him an admiration for your beauty and virtue such as befits a prince towards a lady of the court, I cannot joy, as you seem to do, in the prospect of the prince's using his favour to trifle with your affections. I held it but a duty to encourage in lord Hamlet such amity toward you as would serve to advance the nobility of our family. But, sister, professions of love are quite another matter. It is no more for Hamlet freely to choose the future Queen of Denmark than for you or I. In this, as in all matters of state, his will is not his own; he is subject to his birth, and may not carve out his own path, as may lesser creatures such as we. His choice must be circumscribed, since on it depends the safety and health of the whole state.

For Hamlet's suit, then, take it as nothing more than a fashion, a desire of the moment; a violet that has blossomed too soon, and whose perfume will be spent before the frost of prudence nip its sweetness in the bud. Even if his love be sincere, though I beg leave to doubt it, it must at all events yield to the voice of that great body, the state of Denmark, of which he will one day be the head.

Consider, then, my dear sister, what loss your honour may sustain, should you listen to his songs of love with too attentive an ear. Suppose you should lose your own heart to him? Or worse still, unlock the chaste treasure of your virginity to his unmastered importunity?

Fear, it Ofelia, my dear sister, fear it. Keep yourself in the rearguard of your own affections; guard yourself from the shot and danger of desire. Undress your beauty, as a chaste maid should, only to the innocuous gaze of the virgin moon. Be wary: fear is desire's best antidote. Repel Hamlet's suit; disclaim his attentions; keep both your virtue and your good name, that you may never live to be a shame unto your loving brother

LAERTES

The Lord Polonius to the Lady Ofelia
June 1049

Ofelia

I was ere you rose this morning from your chamber dispatched by his majesty our noble King Amled on urgent business to Norway. The matter on which I would confer with you cannot however await my return.

So to be brief. It is told to me that very oft of late the lord Hamlet hath given you freely of his private time, and that you of your audience have been most free and bounteous. If it be so, as so 'tis put on me, and that in way of caution, I must tell you that you do not understand yourself so clearly as befits my daughter, and your own honour.

If you believe prince Hamlet's tenders of affections, then you behave like a green girl, unacquainted with the manners of the world. You may think yourself little more than a baby to accept as true currency protestations that can be no more then thin air. Lord Hamlet is a prince out of your star: as far above you in eminence as my judgement out-tops yours. When Hamlet comes to wed, the match will be one set between nations, not persons; its purpose to seal amity between states, not to fulfil a silly maiden's idle dreams.

Were you to succumb under the sway of these blandishments that pass for love to unchastity, you would dishonour me, my good name and my worth in the eyes of my sovereign. Think on it: the king's chief counsellor father to the prince's drab, grandsire to his unlawful bastard? For shame, Ofelia, for shame. Entertain no more talk or correspondence with the Lord Hamlet. I forbid it as your father

POLONIUS

Prince Hamlet to the Lady Ofelia
April 1050

I know not why, my lady, you should seek to return to me letters I never writ, or remind me of remembrances that come new to my memory. Why indeed should you believe you owe me anything, since I am sure I never gave you aught?

'Tis true that the fishmonger,your father, hath often sung in the market the praises of his mermaid daughter, half-fish, half-flesh; but for my part, touching fish, I cannot abide the stench of 'em. If the sun breed maggots in a dead dog, being a good kissing carrion, then do not walk i' the sun; for though conception is a blessing, 'tis not how you would wish to conceive.

I know you fair; I would you were honest. If you be honest and fair, then your honesty should admit no discourse to your beauty, for the power of beauty will sooner transform honesty into a bawd than the force of honesty can transform beauty into his likeness.

Say I did love you once: why, you should not have believed me. Virtue cannot inoculate our nature from the disease of original sin: cure our rotten carcasses as we may, we will stink of it. Get thee to a nunnery, go. Why wouldst thou be a breeder of sinners? If thou dost marry, I'll give thee this plague for thy dowry: be thou as chaste as ice, as pure as snow, thou shalt not escape calumny. If thou wilt marry, marry a fool, for wise men know what monsters you make of them. To a nunnery, go, and quickly too. Farewell.

HAMLET

Beneath these pages lay another letter, addressed to his dead uncle, his Mother's brother, and written immediately following the death of Polonius

From Fortinbras to the Lord Laertes
June 1050

My noble friend

Though preoccupied with my successful affairs here in Poland, let me yet take time to commiserate, as one who knows what it is to lose a father, on your late bereavement. Knowing, from intelligence, that you bear no love to the Lord Hamlet, I will be so honest and even with you as to speak openly, what is only rumoured in Denmark: that your father's executioner was none other than your former friend the mad prince. They say further that he who set the lunatic on, was none other than his highness King Claudius himself.

Being, in feeling, as it must surely seem also to you, closely allied to your loss (for my father too died by the hand of one who bears your father's murderer's name) I am so bold as to venture that, were we to meet on this ground, I doubt not some noble enterprise of vengeance would, from that conjoining, issue boldly forth. I know his majesty King Claudius will be sending to you, protesting his innocence of the deed, and blaming Hamlet's madness. Yet, though I have little doubt as to whose hand it was that cut the slender threads of your father's life, we may yet make a shrewd guess at the identity of him who supplied the weapon.

Beware then, dear Laertes, of returning in rash isolation to Helsingor, where you may too easily fall into the trap that swallowed good old Polonius. This very night I march direct from here to Denmark. If thou wilt let the fellow that brings thee these news conduct thee safely to a secret meeting place I have appointed, not far from Helsingor, I have the means to furnish thee readily with arms, and to provide thee with strong and loyal fellows to bear them in this your quarrel, that I am willing to make also mine.

Yet there is a prudence too in these my preparations. For though I hold Claudius guilty in this, yet I allege him guilty only insofar as I count my strength capable of challenging his. It may well be that, meantime, the mad Hamlet should be our stalking-horse; for if we dispatch him, we do Claudius a service he will be bound to reward, and rid him of his heir. Though with my present strength I would fear the outcome of an assault upon Denmark, my threatening might be sufficient to persuade Claudius to look favourably upon good Laertes as his next successor.

I have other designs to lay before thee, but let them remain for your own ears' hearing, Your friend

FORTINBRAS

The boy ceased reading, but did not look up from the table. Chin cupped in his hands, he continued to stare at the manuscript with sightless eyes that gradually filled up with tears.

Seeing that he had finished, Horatio's gentle voice broke silence to complete the story: the part played by Fortinbras in his father's death, and his eager seizing of Denmark's crown; of the manner of his birth, and his mother's death; of the loyal army that had all these years endured the inhospitable climate of Iceland, awaiting the opportunity of regaining their kingdom, and restoring to his rightful inheritance their beloved Lord Hamlet's son, grandson of their great King Amled.

Horatio had returned from the window to his original place on the opposite side of the table. Still unable to look up, the boy was aware of his placing something on the table before him. Slowly raising his eyes, he saw that it was a sword, its long steel blade elaborately damascened with patterns of silver, its hilt encrusted with brilliant gold, set with five bright, iridescent gems.

'You are the son of Hamlet', said Horatio, in the same

gentle voice. 'You are Prince of Denmark. Your people wish you to take the name Sigurd, who was the son of Seigmund, and who took revenge for the killing of his father. Your destiny is also to avenge your father, and to regain your throne. Our ship is ready. We leave for Iceland on the morrow'.

O vengeance. Thy commandment all alone shall live. Now to my word.

It is said that when King Volsung of Hunland erected a great hall, he ingeniously ordered that it should be built around the circumference of a massive oak tree. Thus it was that the roots of the tree formed the hall's foundations, and its roof-timbers were the tree's topmost branches. The oak's great trunk was the building's central pillar and its leafy branches budded out through the windows. To the trunk men gave the name 'Branstock'.

One night while the Volsungs sat around their fires beneath the shelter of the living oak-timbers, there entered a stranger into the hall. Beneath his ragged cloak his feet were bare. When he threw back his hood, revealing a face worn with antiquity, he glared on the company from only one good eye, the other being wrinkled and shut with blindness. In his hand he grasped a sword. Before any man could draw a weapon, with amazing force he struck the sword into the trunk of the tree, so that it sank up to the hilts in the wood. Then he said:'Let he who is brave enough to draw the sword from this oak, take and keep it as a gift from me. He will find, in truth, that he has never held a better'. Then he vanished from the hall, and no man knew whither he had gone.

All the Volsungs were eager to try the sword, for all coveted it, and each man believed himself the strongest and bravest of the company. All tried, but none could draw the sword from where it stuck fast; though they tugged and pulled, they could not loosen it from the oak.

Then last of all Sigmund, son of King Volsung, set his hand to the sword and easily drew it forth. Others of the tribe protested, claiming that Sigmund was not the noblest among them, and could not claim any of their prowess in war. Some offered to buy the sword for thrice its weight in gold. But Sigmund replied:'Any one of you could have drawn this sword from the Branstock, had it been your lot to bear it. But now none else shall take it, for, as my destiny, its possession has fallen to me'.

FROM THE VOLSUNGA SAGA

Part five

1

Holy Island

July 1065

he night after Horatio's arrival, the dreams began.
They were, from the outset, quite unlike ordinary
dreams, having nothing of the arbitrariness, the jumbled
images and discontinuous narratives of a familiar reverie.
Nor did they present the usual rapprochement of the
strange and the everyday, where the accidents of the previous day's occurrences consorted with revived ancestral
memories, and visions of an undreamed of future. Everything that appeared in these dreams was tactile to the
senses, vivid to the imagination. The story they told, or
the drama in which they implicated him, pressed on
towards some great or terrible denouement, some outcome both fearsome, and hungrily desired.

The boy – or as Horatio had now identified him, the
young prince – found himself, in his dream, standing high
on battlements that rose precipitous from the edge of a
cliff-face overhanging the sea. Though it was night, he
could clearly see his surroundings by a light that was
more than the cold glow of a low-hanging moon, trailing
tracks of white luminosity across the surface of black
and silent waters. The rampart on which he stood was

fashioned from stones so massive that they seemed more like mysteriously eroded outcrops of natural rock than the work of human hands. Resting on the rough stone ledge, his fingers felt, with a dream-like exaggeration, their deep age, and read in their worn and weathered, notched and knobbed contours the cryptic language etched on their surface by the past they had witnessed. Across the narrow stretch of dark water, candid moonlight fringed rugged edges of crag and cliff, the coastline of Sweden. The dribbled trail of white phosphorescence left by the moon led the eye along that inscrutable shore towards the sharp point of Skalderviken, then onwards to the straits between Skagen and Goterborg, and out towards the Skagerrak and the open sea. Beyond lay the vast waters of whale and walrus, the frozen tundra and glacial wastes of the north, a harsh and forbidding passage through which a man, hardy enough in strength and sufficiently firm in purpose, could pass, to find the whole immense world, the earth and the waters under the earth, lying enticingly open to him. From below rose the soughing and chafing of the sea. The air bit shrewdly.

He found himself moving down a spiral stone staircase, repetitively circling a massive black column, drawn unresisting downwards into an unfathomable blackness. Torches, hung in iron brackets on the walls, sputtered and flared, fitfully illuminating trickles of running water. Their brightness was reflected in the dark sheen of wet stone, and cast grotesque patterns across the stippling of lichen and moss on the walls.

At length he was at the bottom of the shaft, glancing

back up to see black, rough-hewn steps disappearing into a torch-lit gloom, peering forward down a tunnel that branched off and sloped gently down into darkness, like the gallery of a mine. Here his passage became more difficult and his dream-feet began to encounter the obstructions of fallen rock and shattered timber, to stumble and stagger in the darkness. Here the air was thick and foul, fetid and pungent with odours of death and decay. Were the piles of accumulated debris that encumbered and arrested his feet the roots of trees, or human bones? Was the pin-point of light that glimmered faintly in the remote blackness a chink of daylight, or the eerie glimmer of a phantom, one such as that seen by his father on those same battlements, an ancient ghost risen from these sepulchral depths to seek again the glimpses of the moon?

Then at last he found himself at the end of the tunnel which opened out to release, to a vivid blue sky, the mountain stream that had joined and accompanied his subterranean journey from the heart of the hills. Over centuries the water had dripped and filtered, run and gathered, patiently worming and working its way through stubborn rock, finally wearing out a passage to the outer air. Now it tumbled over a smooth lip of rock, plummeting down a hundred feet or more into the tight declivity of a gorge. Far below he could see where the falls foamed into a rocky basin and from there bounced and buffeted their way towards the green valley far below.

Now he was at the foot of the fall, his feet sliding and slipping on wet boulders, above him the spring bursting violently out from the rock-face, cascading with impossible precipitation, a solid column gleaming in the spring sunshine. Behind the fall, where it dropped into the basin, he could see, through a mist of spray, the mouth of a cave, overhung by a lip of rock on which grew a bright green fur of moss. Tapering funnels dangled over the rim, dripping trickles of splashed water into the pool. From the cave's darkness glowed a faint radiance. In his ears reverberated a strange music, cadences rippling with the rhythm of the stream, harmonies that mingled with the clatter and splash of water on rock, notes that rang with the plangent melody of softly blown horns. The rising sun caught a fine spume of mist that drifted across the cave's mouth, turning and refracting the mingled colours of the spectrum. His dream-self floated, gliding easily, over that rainbow-bridge, drawn downwards into darkness, towards promise and fear.

This was the end. Roof and floor of the cave closed together to a sharp edge as if the space were a wedge driven deep into the mountain's heart. At the narrowest point lay a rough stone block, like a sacrificial altar. On it lay a long slim object, tightly swathed and bound in a covering of some fine material. The faint phosphorescence of light with which the cave glowed came from within the covering, from whatever lay wrapped in that linen shroud. Instinctively the prince's fingers felt at the bonds, pulled at a tie, loosened a knot and divested the thing of its wrappings. On the altar lay a sword, much like that presented to him by Horatio, but infinitely brighter and more beautiful. The sheen of light on its keen blade was blinding, and the coloured gems set into its golden hilt filled the soul with the hungry ache men feel at the sight of some unbearable loveliness. His dream-hand seized its handle and held its keen point towards the light. It lay easily, as if it had always lain there, in his hand.

He stood at the mouth of the cave, behind him the rainbow of mist, bright sword gleaming in his hand, and traced with his eye the course of the stream that chased away across green meadows to the *fjord* and the open sea. It was time to begin his journey. He could feel the distinct presence of someone, or something, observing him.

2

At sea

July 1065

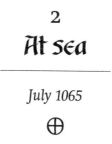

I t was not long, however, before the young prince's whole experience, day by day, began to assume the character of a dream. His familiar surroundings were left behind so suddenly and completely that his very life became, overnight, a remote recollection. He was like one who, having lost his own memory, is become a stranger to himself. So it was, with not only an assumed name, but with what seemed another's eyes, and with a sensibility new-born, that he observed the increasingly strange contours of a new world come floating towards him out of the morning sea-mists. Yet a sense of awakened wonder, that came from his old and innocent self, also never entirely left him.

For hours he would stand alone in the prow of the black dragon-ship, listening to the flapping and furling of the gently bellying sail, or to the soft slap of the oars when the wind had dropped, and watch the fabled lands and seas of the north, buried deep in his blood from saga and song, solidify from myth and legend into tangible reality. The ship hugged the Northumbrian coast to its northernmost point, skirted the Orkneys, then steered across the straits to the Faroerne. Nothing in Sigurd's dreams ever resembled the strangeness, once they had threaded the islands, of that final exit from the narrow sound into the Atlantic, leaving astern the huge wall of rock that loomed behind them in the shadowless midnight twilight.

But his first glimpse of Iceland seemed to him like nothing else in the world for its fierce and forlorn beauty. It was a dark morning of storm and rain, with a solid blackness behind them out to sea, and ahead the sun rising very bright, under a black canopy of cloud, over the land. As they began to follow the coast to the west, the boy gazed in astonishment at the immense glacier of Vatna-jokull, where rivers of ice seemed to run right down into the sea, their grey translucence beginning to sparkle in the early sunlight. Between them lay desolate black beaches of volcanic rock and sand, and beyond the glacier, sharp peaks, some black and snow-flecked, others sheathed in a skin of pure ice, now beginning, as the clouds dispersed, to stand out in distinct relief in the pure air, hard and beautiful against the vivid and intense cobalt blue of the Arctic sky. He saw the towering cone of Oroefajokull, with only a faint drift of smoke hinting at the volcanic turbulence and power that lay at its heart. In the evening, over these heart-rending sights the sun set with a watery, copper-and-green splendour; but then did not, as he expected, disappear beneath the rim of the world, but clung to the horizon, continuing the night long to emit a weird and unearthly twilight.

They went ashore at Kaflavik, and immediately began to march inland, following the southern shore of the Hafnarfjord. Already acclimatised to wonder, the boy paid but scant attention to the clouds of steam and smoke that burst from the ground, and the pervading stench of sulphur that made him feel he was skirting some grim outpost of the infernal regions. As they trekked eastwards, they passed a lava desert, grey and gravelled, strewn with misshapen lumps of rock. Not a single tree broke the desolate monotony of the plain that seemed again like a piece of the underworld, flung by a deep geological trauma to the earth's surface.

In this harsh world. Craters and lava domes displayed the wounds of cracks and fissures. Everywhere the same barren landscape, on which nothing grew but scrubby moss and lichens, struggling to find life on the black lava. Far off, the cone of Keiler stood out beyond the stark lavafields of Strandarheidi.

Draw thy breath in pain. By the time they reached their appointed shelter at Rekyavik, the boy was so travel-weary that the sleep he dropped into seemed dreamless as death.

Nonetheless the shapes of mountain and volcano, glacier and waterfall, white snow-bound ridge and black lava desert, moved continuously under his consciousness, as though the mind's journey still proceeded, though the body was at rest.

3
Iceland

July 1065

By noon on the following day they had reached their final destination, and Sigurd was staring round him in awe-struck fascination at the valley of Thingvellir. This truly was another world. Between the tall cliff of the Logberg and the broken lava ramparts that sloped down to the lake shore, an immense square platform of dark volcanic rock was thrust up from the earth to form a natural rostrum. The boy stood, open-mouthed, on the platform's surface, taking in his surroundings. Above him the craggy pinnacle of the Logberg towered into the sky. Below, the floor of the valley was covered with vivid green grass, which, nibbled close by wild mountain goats, gave an incongruent impression of cultivation. Across the glittering blue waters of the lake, black peaks were humped under white clouds.

Horatio pointed out to him the features of the place,

explaining how it was used for meetings of the *Althing*[*]. This very day, the summer solstice, was the time appointed for such an assembly. Soon the chiefs would be arriving with their retinues to take part. As they spoke, the boy made some inquiry about a distant object, and pointed with his right hand towards the south-east.

It was in this attitude that the old Viking chief Thorsten first saw him, as he emerged into the valley at the head of his long column of armed men which was threading the pass under the Logberg. The sight of that slight, blonde figure, black cloak flapping around his shoulders, pointing towards the distance where lay his homeland, unseen these fifteen years, was like a blow to the old man's heart. He clambered onto the platform, flung his arms round Horatio and turned to the young prince. As he perceived the unmistakable resemblances in the young face to both father and mother, he dropped to his knees and seized the boy's hand, covering it in kisses. Then he bent his head to the ground so that his forehead rested in obeisance on the prince's foot.

Sigurd became aware, during this ceremonial greeting, of other men entering the valley, arriving from different directions, all gravitating towards the platform. Tens, then hundreds, and finally thousands of armed men were filling the valley, lining the natural ramparts by the lake-shore, clustering and clambering around the slopes and pinnacles of the Logberg. All were as Sigurd had seen them depicted in illustrations and tapestries, tall and fair-

[*] Assembly of all the island's communities

haired; all with heavy moustaches, some with fierce jutting beards; all wearing short coloured tunics, each with the badge of his clan, a wolf, or an eagle, or a hawk. All wore metal helmets of different design: some a simple conical casque with nose-guard, others with face-plates such as he had seen in pictures of Greek armour; some plain, some richly decorated with gilding and ornamental metalwork. Some wore surcoats and leggings of chainmail, others went bare-armed and bare-legged. All lightly and readily handled their weapons, axe and sword, spear and shield.

Every man stood quietly, waiting for his companion to find a place; and all stared, with one gaze, at the young prince, as he stood on the rock platform, the old Viking chief still prostrate before him. Thingvellir was filled with a silence so profound that the lapping of waves on the shores of Thingvallavatn, and the flurry of winds that chased one another through the crags, were the only audible sounds.

Thorsten rose to his feet, his gaze still fixed on the boy. Then he stepped back, drawing his sword in a graceful continuous movement that swept it high into the air above his head, and cried, in a voice that echoed from the Logberg and reverberated around the lake-shore, the single word: 'Sigurd!'

Immediately a forest of swords, spears, axes and knives seemed to grow from the thickly serried ranks of men, and a deep-throated roar deafened the ear. Horatio drew Hamlet's sword from under his cloak and placed it in Sigurd's hand. The boy looked around him at the crowd of roaring warriors and following the example of Thorsten, instinctively raised his own weapon, the blade catching the vertical rays of sunlight and weaving a rainbow of light in the air. The sight of Prince Hamlet's sword silenced the army. Thousands of men fell to their knees in homage before the raised sign of their lost, loved prince. The boy slowly turned in a circle, keeping the sword held high above his head. He could feel the strength of that great army flow through his body, down his arm, into his sword, making both the weapon and its wielder invincible, invulnerable, unconquerable. Then again, instinctively, he pointed with his other hand towards the south east. Again the warriors were on their feet, rattling their weapons against their shields, roaring their proud battle-cries, threatening death to their old enemy, swearing to die rather than live any longer in exile. Shouts of 'Sigurd!' mingled with other names just as loudly proclaimed: 'Amled!' 'Hamlet!'; 'Thorsten!'. Gradually the ragged thunder of shouted names became a continuous repetition of one word, the name of their homeland: 'Denmark!'

The boy kept his position, pointing in the same direction, bright sword raised above his head, while the thunder of the crowd persisted unabated. Now to my word.

Armed with his sword, Gram, Sigurd went forth to slay the great worm, Fafnir. First he sought the monster by the cliffs where he came to drink. Cunningly Sigurd buried himself in the mud of the watering-place, so that the dragon would neither see nor smell his presence.

Then Fafnir came down to drink, and the earth shook with the weight of his passage. From his snarling jaws he hurled poison at every living thing that came near him. Sigurd was not afraid at the monster's roaring and held his position. Fafnir lay down to drink and his belly covered the hole where Sigurd lay. Without hesitation the hero thrust upwards with his sword and ripped into the dragon's vitals.

Scrambling out of his hole, Sigurd beheld Fafnir lashing his great tail in the agony of his death-wound. 'Who are you?' he asked of the man, 'and who was your father? Of what kin do you come, that you dare to bear weapons against me?'

Sigurd replied: 'No man knows my lineage. I have neither father, nor mother. I came into this world alone, and alone I came to seek out you, and to have your life'.

'You lie', replied Fafnir, 'and no true hero would lie to one who is facing death. No nameless man could have vanquished the greatest dragon of all the world'.

'Very well', replied Sigurd. 'I am called Sigurd, and my father was Sigmund'.

'Then am I killed by a noble knight, who is descended from a great father. And hereafter you shall be called Sigurd Fafnirsbana, because by your hand I met my death. So I will share in your memory'.

And with that Fafnir the great worm, the last of his kind, died at the hands of a hero.

FROM THE VOLSUNGA SAGA

The boy stood on the lip of the cone and stared down into hell.

For hours they had pressed up the steepness of Oroefa-jokull, soon leaving the green lower slopes behind; climbing a track that threaded between the successive ice-waves of the glacier; then dragging up the last climb through choking dust of lava deposits that kept the volcano's peak clear both of vegetation and of ice. Keen blasts swung around the summit and whipped into motion little whirlwinds of the black dust, causing eyes to water and throats to parch with dryness.

At last they had reached the summit and stood on the narrow rim of the volcano. Currents of hot air wafted up from the crater, bearing clouds of sulphurous gas. The interior was a great darkness, with the occasional fissure opening to emit bubbles of gas and puffs of black smoke. As his eyes grew accustomed to the darkness of the interior, Sigurd began to perceive flashes of dull heat, as the bubbling lava turned and twisted into momentary visibility through the fracturing and re-forming crust of cooling rock. It resembled, he thought, the opening and closing of many eyes.

Horatio had told him little of their purpose, except to explain that this was a ceremony of some importance, and that though they themselves would have no part to play in it, they were expected to be present. He reminded the boy that these Danes, his people, had, like the Israelites in Egypt, tended to forgot their God, and some had reverted to older beliefs. Once they had recovered their territories, it would be a simple matter to bring them back to the Holy Church. But in the meantime, if they derived courage from the worship of idols, it would be foolhardy, even dangerous, to remonstrate with them.

Horatio's explanations seemed to the prince not entirely free from some degree of embarrassment. Sigurd noticed that his mentor held little converse with the silent Viking who led the procession, dressed in a strange ceremonial cloak sewn with ravens' feathers, his neck circled with a necklace made from the pelts of wolf and of bear. Nor, he also noticed, did Horatio look at the young slave-woman who was led, white and silent, by a chain slipped into her serf-collar, behind the priest. The boy had, of course, seen very few women, accustomed as he was to monastic life; hence it seemed entirely natural to him that any religious ceremony would be undertaken by men alone. It was all the more puzzling, therefore, that a woman should accompany them and he took no little interest in her bare white arms and the curving breasts that swelled the front of her long white mantle. But Horatio's guardedness discouraged him from making any inquiry.

All save the priest knelt on the lip of the volcano; the woman, who seemed bewildered or senseless with fear, was pushed to her knees. Stretching out his arms, the priest began his incantation, speaking in a language the boy did not understand. From the continuous stream of words he picked out the names of the old Norse gods he had read of: Father Odin, Warrior Thor, Mother Freya.

Another word that was repeated frequently so that it seemed somehow central to the ceremony was the name 'Midgard'. Each time this word was pronounced, all looked down into the darkness of the crater, as if expecting to behold some apparition.

As the prayers grew louder and faster, building in a crescendo to approach a climax, the woman began to shudder. Sigurd saw that her eyes were tightly closed, and her whole body racked with a spasm of trembling. The chain had been loosed from her collar and two warriors had crept close to her, where she knelt at the feet of the priest, each placing a hand on one of her shoulders.

The incantation ceased; the priest's arms stretched skywards, then fell abruptly to his sides; the slave-girl's eyes and mouth flew wide open together. But before she could utter the scream caught in her throat, the warriors had thrust her off the ledge and into the crater. Sigurd watched the white-clad body fall, head first, with agonising slowness, into the abyss. Far below them she landed on a black crust of lava, but her screams of terror were drowned in the volcano's thunderous mutterings. Then the rock she lay on slipped sideways, and with a sudden spurt and flare of flame as her dress caught alight, she rolled into the dull glowing heat of the molten core. With a flicker of dark fire and a blast of smoke, like the hoarse grunt of some Leviathan, the volcano had swallowed her, and its black surface settled again into apparent solidity.

Wide-eyed in astonishment, Sigurd looked up at Horatio, wondering what foul ritual this could be. What was it but the offering of blood to a demon? Horatio, aware of the boy's inquisitive glance, did not return his gaze. He too had observed the ceremony with a Christian's trained abhorrence of idol-worship and human sacrifice. But he also saw the rite, as if through the eyes of every other man there, as an offering to a pantheon of gods older, darker, and perhaps – who knows? – ultimately stronger than the one God of Israel.

And, he thought defiantly, if his loyal warrior companions, many of whom were fated to destruction, needed Odin to give them a fair wind to assist their passage; or wanted the power of Thor's hammer to help them smite their enemies; or would need, if the chances of battle fell against them, Freya to dispatch her Valkyries to carry their slain bodies to Valhalla – who should gainsay them? And for all his revulsion, Horatio could understand the grim power-worship that prompted these men, loving husbands and fathers, to toss a defenceless woman into the mouth of Midgard. He too had glimpsed the red and gold scales of the great serpent that lay coiled in the volcano, twisting and turning in the crater, as he opened his flaming jaws to swallow down the welcome gift.

Yet still, Horatio breathed a silent prayer for the poor girl's soul and crossed himself with instinctive reverence in the presence of death. He fervently hoped that merciful God would catch her soul and snatch it from the jaws of the demon. But he and his prince would have need, on this coming enterprise, of a power that could afford no mercy, grant no forgiveness. And if such strength and hardness were to be acquired, as his countrymen believed they could, from that ancient enemy that coiled its length through the heart of the mountain, then Horatio incongruously prayed that they might, indeed, have offered to the world-serpent an acceptable sacrifice.

All the way along the curving bay, flickering torches dotted the darkness. Under a rack of clouds, a low moon touched with cold whiteness the running surge, and silhouetted the black prows of a hundred dragon-ships, riding gently at anchor, their plunging necks and carved, gaping jaws urging onwards towards the open sea. Men splashed in and out of the water, carrying weapons and supplies, shipping oars, hoisting sails.

Their preparations were almost complete, and the voyage that was to take them back to the homeland they had fled so many years before, there to win again their lost territories, or to die bravely on their native soil, was about to begin. The young Sigurd sat on the deck of his own ship, his cloak furled tightly about him against the deepening cold. The ship had been built here, on Iceland, and had never until now touched water. It had been designed and crafted for one purpose: to bear the grandson of Amled back to his kingdom.

The boat was manned by a hand-picked crew of veteran sailors, and carried a group of warriors now sworn to allegiance as Sigurd's *heorthwerod*. In an elaborate ceremony each man in turn had sworn homage to the prince, vowing to protect him against all perils, and to die rather than see him harmed. By this ritual they were freed from allegiance to their own lords, and committed solely to the service of their new prince. Horatio, wanting Sigurd to understand the gravity of this obligation, and the nature of the power to which he was acceding, explained that the function of the *heorthwerod* was purely to protect his life. They would leave a field of battle, where their comrades were dying, to save their lord; but they would not leave that field after their lord had fallen, unless it were to live a life of disgrace and exile. They would fight against their former protectors, if the paramount principle of the prince's safety required; and they would immediately and without question kill any man or woman at the prince's order.

Now these warriors, all dressed in black tunic and cloak, decorated with the silver motif of the Danish crown, superimposed upon a simple cross, who kept an almost priestly silence, as if over-awed by the dignity of their high bond of service, were settling themselves down on the deck to sleep through as much as they could of the long voyage.

The fleet was ready. As if to encourage their departure, a stiff and icy blast swept down from the mountains and bellied the sails. With a creaking of ropes and a slapping of sailcloth, the great fleet slowly moved along the *fjord* and towards the open sea. Lulled by the gentle surging rhythm of the boat as it crossed the calm waters of the sound, Sigurd slept.

4
At sea

August 1065

H e woke, and through the eerie bright darkness saw, directly ahead of him, a huge low moon, its white surface ruptured by marks like the mould of decomposition. The boat was becalmed, the sail dangling limply from the mast, and there was no sound of oars plying the unruffled waters. A strange silence enveloped the craft, as if it were a deserted hulk, floating away from a battle with all its crew slaughtered, or a plague-ship abandoned after the outbreak of some decimating pestilence.

He looked around and saw the humped and muffled shapes of his companions lying as if dead or deeply drugged. The rowers slumped over their oars, the steersman was flopped across his tiller. Ahead and astern, to port and to starboard, the dark waters stretched as far as the eye could see, with no sign of another sail, no glimpse of mast or beaked prow.

Then Sigurd became aware of an unfamiliar shape, crouching before him in the boat's prow; a figure, clad in white, which sat with head bowed over arms, and arms clasped around knees, and with long dark hair cascading around its shoulders. Who was it? What was it? As the boat pitched and rose on the waves, the figure was thrown athwart the moon's surface and appeared haloed by the great white globe, then dropped again into the darkness. From the motionless shape emanated low mutterings of rhythmic sound.

He tried to speak to it but only noises of no meaning escaped his numbed lips. The apparition slowly rose towards him, and he flinched in horror when he recognised the slave-girl sacrificed to Midgard, her white skin seared by disfiguring burns, her eyes shining with a dull glow like pieces of polished basalt, white lips moving in a low, monotonous chanting.

> 'Mighty is Midgard, perfect his power.
> Mighty is Midgard, great is his force.
> His spine is the rock at the heart of the earth.
> His tail is entwined in the Yggdrassil's roots.
> His voice is the thunder,
> The lightning his anger;
> Fire from the ground is the breath of his mouth.
> His jaws are the earth that swallows us down.
> Mighty is Midgard, perfect his power,
> Mighty is Midgard, great is his force.'

Sigurd shut his eyes against the horror and tried to deafen his ears against the maddening repetition. Presently the chanting ceased. When he opened them again, the woman was standing before him, and she was changed. Now she smiled on him, and her face he had known in dreams as the face of his mother, the bright and beatific face of an angel. She stood with the great moon behind her and held out her white-clad arms. Her hair clung wetly to her cheeks, as if she had just emerged from the drowning pool of Drekkingarhylur by Thingvellir, where mothers without husbands were thrown to their deaths. Overjoyed to find her, he sank into her embrace, burying his face in the fresh wetness of her dress, nuzzling like a suckling infant at the receptivity of her breasts.

She cupped his chin in her hands, lifted his face towards her and kissed him on the lips. The kiss was of an indescribable sweetness, but somewhere beneath the sweetness, a faint odour of decay. Lost in the woman's embrace, he felt her tongue wriggle into his mouth, like the flickering tongue of a serpent. Swooning in sensation, he could yet taste poison, and the smell of decay grew stronger. Opening his eyes he saw again the eyes of the slave-girl, glowing with a dull passion. Her white lips fastened hungrily on his, the slippery root of her tongue remorselessly probing the inside of his mouth.

He thrust her from him in a shudder of revulsion, choking with disgust. His face and hands seemed caught in the folds of her white dress, which now were like soft muslin, and now like sour grave-clothes. Helplessly he struggled to break free.

Then he woke, trembling and catching his breath, to see again the familiar deck of the ship with the reassuring shapes of his sleeping retainers. He heard the creak and splash of oars, and saw all around him, in the starlit darkness, the gaping dragon-mouths of the fleet, urging ever forwards on the track of the moon. For a long time he could not shake off the emotion of his nightmare; but after a time the calm, efficient purposefulness of the enterprise that surrounded him, and the soothing onward rhythm of the boat's passage, rocked him again to sleep, and he dreamed again.

A man stood on a hill, dressed all in white, shading his eyes from the hot sun. He was speaking to a great crowd of people who sat or stood around the slopes of the hill. His voice was low and gentle, yet full of strength and love.

'Ye have heard that it hath been said, thou shalt love thy neighbour, and hate thine enemy.

'But I say unto you, love your enemies. Bless them that curse you. Do good to them that hate you. Pray for them which despitefully use you, and persecute you; that ye may be the children of the father which is in heaven.'

WAR IN HEAVEN

And there appeared a great wonder in heaven, a woman clothed with the sun, and the moon under her feet, and upon her head a crown of twelve stars.

And she being with child, cried, travailing in birth, and pained to be delivered.

And there appeared another wonder in heaven, and behold a great red Dragon, having seven heads, and ten horns, and seven crowns upon his heads,

And his tail drew the third part of the stars of heaven, and did cast them to earth: and the Dragon stood before the woman which was ready to be delivered, for to devour the child as soon as it was born.

And she brought forth a man child, who was to rule all nations with a rod of iron: and her child was caught up unto God, and to His throne.

And the woman fled into the wilderness, where she hath a place prepared of God, that they should feed her there a thousand, two hundred, and threescore days.

And there was war in heaven, Michael and his Angels fought against the Dragon, and the Dragon fought and his angels,

And prevailed not, neither was their place found any more in heaven.

And the great Dragon was cast out, that old serpent, called the Devil and Satan, which deceiveth the whole world: he was cast out into the earth, and his angels were cast out with him.

FROM THE REVELATION OF
ST JOHN THE DIVINE

There was another hill, and the same man was nailed to a cross. In the crowd that clustered around the slopes of the hill, there were those who mocked him; and those who stood and watched in silence; and there were those who wept.

Sigurd saw himself standing among them, at the very foot of the cross, and he was of those that wept. The man looked down at him, and his face was the face he had always imagined as that of his own father.

'Forgive them', he said, 'for they know not what they do'.

And the boy found himself saying in reply:

'Father: into thy hands I commend my spirit'.

Then at last, at the very end of his long dream-journey, Sigurd found himself once again atop the battlements of Helsingor. It was a great relief finally to have reached his destination. On the ramparts that surmounted the over-hanging crags, high above the surging and crashing of the waves, he saw a young man, dressed in black, leaning against the battlements, and staring out to sea.

When he approached him, the man turned towards him with a smile of great sweetness, with eyes soft with tenderness, and alight with understanding.

'Put up thy sword into the sheath', he said gently. 'The cup which my father hath given me, shall I not drink it?'

He put his arm around the boy's shoulder, and both looked out to sea.

'A new commandment I give unto you' he said, softly and easily: 'that you love one another. As I have loved you'.

He leaned down and kissed the boy on the forehead, and his kiss was like the touch of peace; then he faded on the crowing of the cock.

5
Helsingor

September 1065

They had bound Fortinbras to a chair, his shoulders pulled back by the tight bonds, his legs flung clumsily forward. White streaks of sweat stood out against the battle-grimed face. Dark blood crusted around the jaw from a gash on his head. Though his face was sullen with exhaustion and hostility, his eyes, undefeated, stared at the young prince as he walked towards him through the ranks of the victorious army.

Throughout the whole long day Sigurd had watched the battle from the deck of his ship, his retainers grouped closely around him, oarsmen ready at a moment's notice to speed away from the scene of battle. Before dawn the advance raiding party had put ashore while the main fleet had ridden the surge behind an unguarded headland. The occasional muffled cry or chink of armour, soon drowned in the great darkness, were the only indications of the Danish presence as the raiders eliminated sentries and pushed forward right up to the castle walls.

Complacent from years of security, Helsingor's defenders had placed little resistance in the invaders' path. The weak points of the castle's defences were exactly remembered by those who used to guard it themselves. A small concealed postern gate broke easily under their levering weapons. A few guards died with expressions of surprise still growing on their astonished faces. Soon the main gates were opened from the inside, while the Norwegians were still dragging themselves from sleep to sound the alarm. Meanwhile part of the fleet had slipped around the promontory and beached its dragon-ships on the shore. Thousands of Danish warriors splashed into the shallow water and, energised by the touch of their native soil, poured up the beach towards the opening castle gates. A substantial force was already inside the castle's perimeters by the time the defenders emerged to give battle. So a skirmish of some hours ensued, the Norwegians attacking the invading force from inner and outer battlements until a strong detachment of guards issued from the gatehouse and began to push the Danes back to the entrance. Assaulted from above by a reinforced defence, the Danes found their forward momentum checked and, taking heavy casualties, fought a hard retreat, inch by inch, back to the open gates. Norwegian attempts to shut the gates against them were however defiantly repelled.

Observing the to-and-fro mêlée from a vantage point on

the headland, Thorsten, the commanding general had to guess at exactly the right moment, when the defenders, judging the invaders to have been repelled with sufficient force from their first attempt, would decide to emerge from the inner defences, to advance and essay a full-frontal attack. Everything depended on that split-second decision, since Thorsten knew that the castle, once properly secured and effectively defended, would be virtually impregnable to even the most well-laid siege. But the experienced old commander selected his moment exactly so that the main body of the fleet, in response to his signal, had rounded the headland and the main invasion force was swarming up the beach, as the Norwegians threw themselves in full strength against their attackers.

The front line of engagement was thus joined just outside the castle's outer wall, and Sigurd was able to observe the obscenity of close-quarter, hand-to-hand fighting. Sickened by the carnage, seeing the world distorted through a red mist of blood, deafened by the howls of wounded and dying men, the prince was hardly aware, except from the rising spirits of his bodyguards, that the Norwegian defences were buckling under the sheer weight of the Danish assault, and that the day was all but won.

As the commingled violence of attack and defence seemed to diminish, the Norwegians pushed back, the invaders feeling the accelerating momentum of a successful advance, a sudden flurry of activity, just outside the castle gates, weapons raised and struck with increasing rapidity and violence, seemed to indicate some decisive precipitation of the battle's fortunes. Though the prince did not at first realise what was happening, warriors of his *heorthwerod* knew that this microcosmic struggle represented the last defensive action of Fortinbras' bodyguard. As the tumult stilled, fighting stopped along the line and a great shout of triumphant joy rose from the invading force as they tasted ultimate victory.

Now Sigurd stood before his captive, the man who had helped to murder his father, the prince who had stolen his birthright. Fortinbras looked back at him, with no sign of fear.

'So, my young prince', he said, speaking with difficulty under the pain of his wounds, 'You are indeed the very copy of your father. Yes, I knew of you, and I sought you, but could never find where you'd been smuggled and hidden. You were always gone, vanished into thin air, before I reached you – always just out of my grasp. I would have picked up your trail, but your servant there was too clever for me. Well, let that be. I concede to your power. My followers I throw on your mercy. Some may wish to stay and serve you. Let the others return to Norway. As a magnanimous prince, show mercy in your triumph. Let my death suffice, and pay the debt for all. I am ready.'

And with a stoic expression, Fortinbras awaited his end.

Horatio stepped forward and clapped the prince's sword into his grasp. Guiding his sword-arm, he placed the point against Fortinbras' throat, then showed the boy how to grip the pommel in his left hand for the thrust.

'Now' he said. 'To your word. Remember your father. Avenge his foul and most unnatural murder'.

King and prince were now a law unto themselves, isolated in the violence of their enmity. The Danish army, fanned out into a long semi-circle around the walls of the castle, awaited the outcome of a combat that would determine the future. It seemed an endless moment, suspended in time, without force or motion, hushed with a great stillness like the silence that reigned in heaven after the opening of the seventh seal.

The boy stood ready, blade pressed tight against Fortinbras's throat, feeling behind him the immense pressure of a national will, the desire of those thousands of warriors, who had endured and suffered so much, for this last fulfilment of all their sacrifices, all their hopes. The prince felt that only by an effort of resistance, from his own slender muscles, could he hold back that tide of human desire.

The victim waited in patience, and without a trace of fear, for the death he fully expected, and to which he was wholly resigned. Fortinbras had lived too long with the arbitrary providence of power to be in any way embittered, or even particularly disappointed, that a turn of fortune's wheel should so easily dislodge him and send him tumbling, as in a matter of minutes he would most assuredly be tumbled, into the unknown. He held the boy's wide-eyed gaze with an ironic and unperturbed expression.

It is finished. Sigurd drew back the blade, as if to add force to his thrust, and jabbed the sword forward. Its point slipped and slid sideways across the king's steel gorget.

He gripped the hilt more tightly, and thrust again. This

time the point nicked Fortinbras' neck, and drew from the tiny cut an insignificant trail of blood.

Fortinbras continued to stare at him in grim amusement. A red rash of frustration coloured the prince's cheeks, and with a hiss of anger he raised the sword high, its blade weaving a bright kaleidoscope of light in the air, and held it poised, ready to cut irresistibly down towards his enemy's head. He noticed Fortinbras' eyes give a momentary flicker. Then he suddenly dropped the sword to his side, turned on his heel, and began to walk, slowly but without hesitation, back towards his waiting ship.

As he walked, the warriors fell back to clear a path for him. At one end of this straight road that opened out before him, he could see the slim curved stern of his boat, tossing in the surf, and on board the black-and-silver figures of his home-troop, now looking alert and concerned. At the other end of the avenue, unseen by the boy, Horatio stood in expressionless silence beside the bound and seated figure of Fortinbras. All watched him go. None broke the silence. It was a long walk.

Ulf Svensson stood in the front rank, and watched the prince pass close to him as he walked. He remembered seeing a young boy, thin shoulders hunched under his cloak, as if he had taken a physical beating, face red with some boyish indignity or shame, lower lip held between his teeth, passing with an almost cringing walk through the ranks of men. He seemed, to Ulf's eyes, to be conscious of having failed a test, and to be walking away from the great chance of his life into the anonymous ignobility of defeat.

Styrbjorn Thorkelsson stood in the front rank, and watched the prince pass close to him as he walked. He recalled seeing a strong young figure, battered but unbroken, bravely and steadily running that long gauntlet of puzzled and disappointed eyes. The prince stared straight ahead, his eyes seeming to register contempt for the easy victory others had won for him. He seemed like some hero of ancient song and story, renouncing a too easy triumph and embarking on a quest to search out some greater challenge, more worthy of his grandfather's noble name.

Asved Tokefostri stood in the front rank, and watched the prince pass close to him as he walked. To him the prince seemed to walk to the shore in quiet serenity, his young face glowing with a light not of this world. With calm and unhurried grace, and a look of eager expectancy, he seemed to turn his back on the ugly scenes of human carnage and conflict and to be advancing joyfully towards the beatific joys of another world.

As Sigurd stepped onto his dragon-ship, the craft scarcely dipping in the water beneath the weight of his slight frame, his home-troop closed behind him and stood, with drawn swords, guarding the stern; and the oarsmen began, without question, to pull out from the shore. Still maintaining their silence, the warriors ran quickly down to the sea's edge to watch the ship depart.

Ulf Svensson saw the prince's *drakkar*[1] pull away from the shore. He saw the boy knelt in the prow, his father's sword held point-down before him, his tearstained face leaning against its hilts, lips moving soundlessly, thin body racked with sobs of disgrace and humiliation.

Styrbjorn Thorkelsson saw the prince's *drakkar* pull away from the shore. He saw the prince kneeling in the prow, holding his father's sword point-downwards before him. His young figure seemed held stiff in the dignity of some high chivalric service, his lips moved as though uttering a vow, and he faced his future with a soldier's patience and determination.

Asved Tokefostri saw the prince's *drakkar* pull away from the shore. He saw the prince kneel in the prow, sword raised like a cross before him. His lips moved in prayer, and his face, touched with unearthly light, radiated a saint-like serenity and acceptance.

Ulf Svensson saw the ship pull strongly out to sea, and disappear into a thick white sea-fog. No-one ever saw it again.

Styrbjorn Thorkelsson saw the ship pull strongly out to sea, and meet a boisterous sea-storm, that tossed it high and low on huge white breakers. The boat then faced the tempest bravely, and disappeared into a bank of thunderous cloud. No-one ever saw it again.

Asved Tokefostri saw the boat pull strongly out to sea.

---

*   'dragon-ship'

He turned to look back, but when his gaze sought for the ship again, it had travelled impossibly far towards the horizon. He blinked in disbelief, and the boat was a distant speck poised on the rim of the world. Asved believed that the prince's dragon-ship had sailed straight over the edge of the earth and into the light of the heavenly kingdom. Certain it is, that no one ever saw it again.

No one ever saw it again. Did it sail away from a defeat, a resignation or a conversion? Was it travelling into failure, adventure or martyrdom?

Was the little craft lost in the curling sea fog, and wrecked on the sharp rocks of some treacherous northern coast? Or overwhelmed and capsized by the heaving seas of a winter storm? Or did the mariners navigate their way beyond the world's rim, to find that fabled land beyond the setting sun, where man would live at peace with himself and his neighbour, and walk familiarly with his God?

The questions began to form, and the legends to grow. Some said the prince was at the bottom of the ocean, and would return no more until the sea gave up her dead. Some said he would come back, in the fullness of time, to reclaim his kingdom, as his grandfather had done, by the strength of his own arm. Some said he had joined the company of the saints in heaven, and would not be seen on earth again until the Lord Himself should return in glory, with his angels and archangels, to judge both the quick and the dead.

Whose kingdom shall have no end. But nobody knew, in absolute truth – neither the crafty counsellor in court, nor the brave hero beneath the blue sky – who, at the last, unloaded that cargo.